# SOUNDS

# OF

# TOMORROW

## DREW BANKSTON

All characters in the book are fictional and any resemblance to actual persons, living or dead, is entirely coincidental.

Copyright © 2023 Drew Bankston
ISBN 978-0-9975547-7-9

http://www.drewbankston.com
All Rights Reserved
Printed in the United States

Cover design by Christi Bankston

# Dedication

Dedicated to my family, both living and dead, who have loved me and shaped me throughout my life and taught me to see my own future as always bright and filled with love.

-Drew

# CHAPTER 1

## GOODBYE

"I'm so excited for today! The martial arts demo is a great way to raise money for neglected and abused children. I hope it's a huge success and we can raise as much money as possible for such an important cause. I've been practicing hard for this and know I will do fantastic," Jessi said to herself in the mirror.

She slipped into her all-black uniform and tied the black belt around her waist. She looked in the mirror and smiled.

"You don't look too bad in black," she chuckled to herself and grabbed her workout bag.

She ran down the stairs and tossed her bag toward the front door. It slid across the floor and stopped with a slight bump just to the right of the door frame. "Strike!" Jessi shouted and did a little dance.

The smell of bacon sizzling in the kitchen made her stomach growl and grumble. She trotted into the kitchen, where her mom put the last few pieces of bacon on the paper towel-covered plate.

"Good morning, Jess," her mom said.

Jessi sat at the table. "Morning! Breakfast smells amazing! Thanks for getting up to make it."

"Of course! My girl has to have energy for her big day!"

Jessi blushed. "It's not *my* big day, mom. It's just a demo in the park. Besides, I'm seventeen years old now. I probably don't even need breakfast anymore."

"Breakfast is good for you at any age," her mom said, cracking some eggs into the frying pan. They sizzled as they hit the hot surface. "It may not be your special day, but today, you can show off your amazing black belt skills," her mom said as she stirred the eggs in the pan to scramble them.

Most of her friends at school knew the Jessi, who was a quiet and easygoing teenager. Few knew the Jessi, who had studied for seven years to become a black belt in Kung Fu. She looked at it as her secret life. A few of her friends knew, but they were the ones who joined her and shared in this other life away from the routine and mundane.

"Is most of your class attending the demo today?" Jessi's mom scooped some eggs onto Jessi's waiting plate.

"I think so," Jessi responded, shoveling a forkful of eggs into her mouth, followed by a bite of bacon. "Are you and Dad coming?" Jessi spoke through the mouthful of food.

"We wouldn't miss it, sweetheart," her mom said. "We're both so proud of you. Are you sure you don't want us to drive you?" Jessi's mom already knew the answer. What seventeen-year-old would want to show up to an event in her parent's car?

"Thanks, but I'll ride the bus with the rest of the school. How about if I ride home with you, though?"

"That sounds good." Jessi's mom grew quiet.

"Everything ok?" Jessi asked and gulped down some milk.

"Everything's fine. Just promise me you'll be careful."

Jessi stopped eating, a forkful of eggs halfway to her mouth. "I'm always careful," she said. "You know that."

I do," her mom said, "but I just have a funny feeling about today. You know how much I hate it when I get these feelings."

"Yeah, I do," Jessi said, trying as hard as she could not to roll her eyes. "And before you say anything, I know about Grandma Vicci and her premonitions. Everything will be fine."

Jessi's mom walked over to her and placed her hand on Jessi's shoulder. "It's a mother's prerogative to be able to worry about her child," she said. "So whether I have a good reason, a bad reason, or no reason at all, I'm allowed to worry about you."

Jessi looked up and said, "And I appreciate it. But I'll be fine. Today will be fine. I'm going to have fun with my friends. I'll be careful, and nothing bad will happen. In fact, I feel like this will be an amazing day! I have so much energy and am in such a good mood. Nothing is going to make this a bad day, Mom!"

Jessi's mom wrapped her in a big hug, kissed her on the top of the head, and walked back to the stove. "Did you want me to drive you to the school?"

"It's a beautiful day out. I think I'll walk. It'll help me digest this wonderful breakfast you made me. I don't want to be too full when the demo starts."

2

"Ok. We'll see you at the demo then. I love you."

Jessi stood up from the table and walked over to her mom, giving her a big hug. "I love you too!" She exited the kitchen and hollered, "See you at the demo!"

She hurried to the front door, grabbed her workout bag, and headed outside. As she quickly walked down the street, she turned back to see her mother standing inside the house, watching her through the window. Even though she couldn't clearly see her face, she imagined her mother looking worried.

# CHAPTER 2

## FRIENDS

It was a short fifteen-minute walk from her house to the school. Jessi was happy, but somewhere in her mind, a small one percent of her consciousness thought about what her mom said about being careful, her feelings, and the insight that grandma once had. The other ninety-nine percent of her mind thought about the upcoming day.

Jessi didn't have siblings, although she had always wished she had a younger brother or sister. She helped with the kid's classes at the Kung Fu school and babysat for neighbors often. She had a kind heart and used her kindness to help whomever she could, wherever she could, and whenever she could.

So today, early on a Saturday, the advanced students of her Kung Fu school were to meet in the school parking lot, in uniform, where a hired bus would take them to the park. And Jessi would be there to help.

The air was crisp this morning, and a slight chill indicated that fall might only be a few days away. It was early September, and in Colorado, that meant that even though fall officially arrived toward the end of the month, the temperatures and trees could indicate an early arrival.

Jessi was fortunate to be involved in a school with several students. As with all groups and most teens, Jessi had her set of close friends. She was among the first students to arrive, so she dropped her bag and sat by the school's front door, watching as students came individually, waiting for her best friends to show up.

Cars pulled up. Students got out, waving their goodbyes to the parents, and wandered to other parts of the parking lot, sitting on the grass or curbs. Most acknowledged Jessi and then wandered off to stretch. Others arrived and immediately went into the now opened building and to the classroom to find weapons to use in the demo to display their abilities. Jessi's friend, Rachel, showed up after being dropped off by her dad. Jessi could see Rachel's dad talking to her and looking worried. She saw Rachel shake her head and place her hand on her father's arm. Rachel nodded, leaned over, and kissed her father on the cheek. After a lot of nodding on Rachel's part and a quick hug, she emerged from the car and quickly walked over to Jessi, turning to give a reassuring smile and wave to her dad as he honked and slowly drove off.

"Hey Jess," Rachel said, smiling as she trotted over to her friend.

"Rachel!" Jessi gave her a hug. "I didn't think your dad would let you participate in these demos. I remember you saying how worried he gets, and from the look of things before you got out of the car, I wasn't sure that he'd let you out."

"Eh, you know my dad," she started. "First, he's all worried that I will get hurt in class, so he pulls me out of the school. Then, after a while, he gets worried that I will get hurt by a guy or girl bully at school or out on a date, so he puts me back in. He can't make up his mind. I know he loves and is concerned about me, so I forgive him." They both chuckled at the sentiment. "But if he had just left me in class, I'd be a black belt like you now and not trailing along as a green belt. I'm glad I have a friend like you who can tutor and help me keep up on things I've missed. Your hints, tips, and private lessons have made me a better Martial Artist."

Jessi felt herself blush slightly. "Dads are strange creatures," she said thoughtfully. "You never know what to think about them. I mean, my dad can be a freak of nature sometimes, too. One day, he's treating me like I'm all grown up, and the next day, he's treating me like a little kid. Go figure."

"Well, if it isn't the dynamic duo!" Another of Jessi's friends, Erin Smith, bounced up to the two girls. "Are we discussing boys, sports, fashion, or school?"

"None of the above, Erin, my dear," Jessi said. "We're actually talking about fathers."

"Ah, I see. I have no comment. My dad wants us to move to New Zealand, so I'm unsure what to think." She shook her head. "New Zealand! Who moves from Colorado to New Zealand? I certainly hope not me. So, let's start over." Erin turned around and walked a few steps away, then turned back, spread her arms, and said, "Jessi!"

"Erin!" Jessi said happily and walked into the other girl's arms, enjoying the hug. Jessi took a step back and whistled. "Wow, look at you all fancy in your black uniform and new black belt. Going to work out with me at the demo? You haven't picked a sparring partner yet, have you?"

"Are you kidding? I wouldn't miss it. You helped me get this by giving me numerous bumps and bruises, so I think a little payback is in order." Erin smiled.

"Yeah, we'll see. I'm just glad you're here," Jessi said, giving her friend another hug.

"So, did you hear about Zane and me?" Erin asked.

"No," Jessi replied, and the three girls huddled together for a conference.

"He sent me a text. A *text* to tell me he was breaking up with me this morning before I left for the demo."

"Are you kidding me?" Jessi asked. "Why would he do that?"

"We weren't getting along lately, so I guess it was mutual. I'm not really that upset about it. In fact, I think he was more afraid of breaking up with a black belt than I would have been breaking up with him." The girls laughed.

Other kids had fun warming up in the parking lot. Jessi watched several of them and then noticed the class show-off, Jake Markley. She nudged Erin and nodded toward him. "I really enjoy martial arts, but I can't believe when people show off like he does. He's always trying to do things he doesn't know how to do and hasn't practiced."

"Yeah," Erin agreed. "He's going to hurt someone someday. It'll probably be him, but I hope it won't be someone else."

The students waited, talked, and anticipated. After what seemed like hours more than minutes, the bus pulled up, and the instructors took head counts, made lists, and packed the cargo holds of the bus.

Ray, the head instructor, whistled loudly to get everyone's attention. "Everyone gather round," he hollered. Ray looked over some papers while the excited students gathered around their head instructor. Ray stepped onto the bus entrance stairs so he could see everyone. "Okay. I think everyone is here. Before we start boarding the bus, I want you all to know how proud I am of you. You are all amazing martial artists and people. I want you all to have fun today. The excitement of the day might tempt you to move a little faster than usual, but just remember that we're not only showing off how well you know self-defense, but we're also showing off your control. I don't want anyone hurt today, so be safe and have fun. Everything is packed into the storage area. It's a twenty-minute ride to the park. If anyone needs to use the restroom, do so now." He paused, and when no one moved, he said, "Okay, team. Let's get on board and go have some fun!"

Everyone cheered and started up the steps of the bus entrance as Ray moved to the top.

After one more headcount while herding the class into the bus, the engine roared to life, the door closed, and they were off.

# CHAPTER 3

## THE RIDE

Once the bus left, everyone knew it wouldn't be long before they arrived at the park. There was chatter everywhere. The excitement was electric. The twenty-minute drive took them over some winding roads through the foothills just outside of town. Most kids sat with their close friends and talked during the ride. Some listened to music on their phones, while others texted their friends who didn't attend the Kung Fu school, inviting them to come to the park and at least watch.

Jessi and Erin sat together. Jessi always liked the window seat. She felt more freedom and less confinement when she sat there. She felt free and safe as she watched the world speed by. And if the conversation hit a slow moment, which it seldom did with Erin, she could always close her eyes, feel the breeze on her face, and pretend she was a super hero flying through the air. She loved nature, trees, and fresh air. Getting out to do anything that included those made her happy. She thought of how the demo would proceed and how it would feel working out on the soft grass.

As with many buses packed with teenagers, this one was filled with noisy chatter, laughter, and pranks. Kids shoved each other and ran through mock moves in their seats. The noise rose in volume when one of the kids started challenging Jake to a dare.

"I bet you can't do it," one student chided. "You can't jump kick and touch the ceiling of the bus. Especially when it's moving."

"I can do that," Jake boasted. "No problem. I've kicked higher than that before. Just watch. I'll show you right now."

Jake got out of his seat and stood in the bus aisle. He grabbed the top of the seats on either side of the aisle and looked at the bus ceiling.

Erin nudged Jessi and nodded toward the back.

"Jake," Jessi shouted out, "sit down! You're going to get hurt!"

"You're just jealous that I'll do something you've never done," Jake yelled out above the chants of the crowd. "Just relax, watch, and learn."

After a silent countdown, Jake pushed himself up, and kicked toward the ceiling. He missed by inches, trying to regain his balance as his feet hit the bus floor. The rocking of the bus traveling along the winding road made it difficult for even the most talented artist to keep their balance, so when Jake landed, he struggled to land without falling on some of the other students or to the floor.

The bus driver looked into his mirror. "Hey! You in the back! You need to sit down, now!"

Jake ignored the demand. Even though his kick was high, it wasn't good enough prevent the boy who dared him from snickering, pointing, or laughing. "Lame! So lame! You call yourself a black belt? My grandma could kick higher than that."

Jake's instructor looked back. "Jake," he said, "Sit down!"

"Okay," Jake said, looking back up at the ceiling and preparing to try again. "One second. I almost had it. Just one last try!"

The bus driver was becoming irritated at what was happening and, looking up in his mirror again, he yelled back, "Young man, you have to sit down or I'm going to pull the bus over and you can walk. Sit down *now!*"

"Okay! Yeah." Jake said. "I've got this. Last time. I can do it."

"No, Jake," the head instructor yelled, standing up from his seat, "you need to sit down now, or you're not going to participate in the demo."

The driver continued to glance up at his mirror and watched as Jake's instructor got up to go back and discipline the young man, grabbing seat backs to keep himself from falling on the winding road. To his horror, the driver looked back down at the road and saw a large truck rounding the curve and crossing the centerline.

The bus driver hit the horn and turned sharply to the right. Although he avoided a head-on collision with the truck, the truck still clipped the back end of the bus, causing it to spin and roll completely over once and landing back upright on the wheels.

The entire event happened slowly to the driver, the instructors, and the kids. Each had that helpless feeling of watching it happen but could not do anything about it. Bodies floated in the air as the bus rotated. Students bodies hit metal ceiling, walls, floor, seats and each other. While the collisions happened, no one felt pain. The whole scene seemed to unfold in an entirely different plane of existence.

At first, no one moved once the bus had stopped its slow roll and was upright again. Then students and the instructors stirred.

"Is everyone okay?" Ray said, pulling himself to a standing position on shaky legs. He went from seat to seat checking each student.

The dazed and bruised bus driver took a deep breath. He would have shaken his head, but it throbbed and spun. He looked up where the mirror once existed, more out of habit than anything. The mirror was gone. He looked to the left and saw the radio. Reaching for the microphone, he radioed for help, opened the door, and still shaking, started helping the students out, one at a time. As noisy as the bus had been just before the crash, the silence that now filled the bus was ominous. Most students were fine. A few had minor cuts and bruises. Many were in shock. The ones that stood and made their way to the front seemed to do so aimlessly.

Erin managed to stay in her seat, but stared straight ahead. She waited for her world to stop spinning and when it finally did, she looked over at Jessi, "That was quite the ride. Are you okay?"

Jessi didn't answer. Erin looked over at her friend. Jessi's eyes were closed, and blood trickled from her head where it had hit the broken window.

Erin yelled, "Help! Somebody help! Jessi!" She turned in her seat and pleaded, "I think Jessi is hurt, and I don't think she's breathing. Someone help, please."

Once again for Erin, time slowed down. She could hear her heart beating and didn't know what was happening when a young man gently lifted her out of the seat, helped her to the front of the bus, and out the door. She could only hear her voice yelling and the blood rushing through her ears, but her yelling sounded far away. She knew she was yelling, but it didn't seem to be coming from her mouth. The man that had taken her from her friend helped her to sit down, and she watched, confused, as they brought Jessi out of the bus on a stretcher and loaded her into a waiting ambulance.

As the world started to make sense once again, Erin looked around and saw paramedics talking with and treating her friends. Then she saw Jake. He was standing in front of one of the instructors. He seemed unscathed. Not a scratch on him. It was as if he hadn't been on the bus at all.

He stood with his head bowed, and Jake's instructor yelled at him. She couldn't hear everything. Just the occasional words like "irresponsible" and "reckless." She stared and glared in Jake's direction until he looked up and right at her. He saw her glare and turned away.

Erin turned to Billy, who was sitting next to her on the grass.

"Are you ok, Billy?"

"I think so. Just shook up. I don't think I've ever seen so many emergency vehicles." He looked around. "Police cars, fire trucks, and ambulances everywhere."

Erin hadn't noticed any of it. Her mind had withdrawn into her own small surrounding. Now that Billy had said something, her world slowly expanded and she became aware. "It looks like they closed the road on either side of the accident," Erin said. "Are those your parents coming through the barricade?"

"Yeah." He waved weakly as his parents frantically made their way to him. "Do you see yours yet?" Billy asked Erin.

"No," Erin strained to see each car coming through.

The paramedics fanned out and tended to each person from the bus and the truck driver, whose truck was not severely damaged, but still, he was shaken up and worried about whether he would get the ticket. One of the paramedic teams came over to Erin and took care of the few cuts that she had, asked for her name, and said they would call her parents. She stood up, felt shaky and unsteady, and sat back down again on the soft grass. She felt that reaching the grass voluntarily was preferable to reaching it unconsciously or losing balance.

She heard cars pulling up and saw parents getting out and looking around to find their children, hugging them, and saying how glad they were that their child was okay. Then she saw a familiar car. It was Jessi's parents. Erin tested her legs, and when convinced they would hold her, she walked over. Jessi's mother looked at her with an uncertain look.

"Erin, are you okay? Where's Jessi?" Jessi's mother's voice shook.

The shock of the accident was beginning to wear off, and Erin started to cry. "I don't know if she's okay," she sobbed, "They took her in the ambulance. She was bleeding and unconscious. She has to be okay. She's my best friend. Oh, mister and misses O'Donnell, I'm so sorry this happened!"

Mrs. O'Donnell's mothering instincts kicked in, and she wrapped her arms around the young girl. "It's not your fault, Erin. I'm sure that Jessi will be okay." But she wasn't sure she believed what she was saying without knowing the facts.

A paramedic rushed over. "Did I hear that you're the O'Donnells?"

Jessi's mother nodded. Her father said, "Where's our daughter? What's happened to her?"

"We've been trying to reach you on the phone. She's been taken to County General. You should go. I'll tell them that you're on your way."

Jessi's mother started to cry and looked at Erin. "Are your parents here?"

Erin shook her head. "They're probably on their way. Please let me know how Jessi is doing."

"We'll let you know as soon as we hear something. Do you have your cell phone?" Mr. O'Donnell asked.

Erin nodded and held up her phone. She mouthed the word, yes, but her throat was tight, and the word just wouldn't come out.

"Come on dear," he said to his wife, putting his arm around her shoulders, "we'd better go."

A police officer heard the conversation and offered, "I can escort you to the hospital so you can get there quickly."

Jessi's dad nodded and said, "Thank you! We'd appreciate it!"

Erin cried. She watched Jessi's parents hurry off. She thought about Jessi. She couldn't get the thought of her leaning lifelessly against the window out of her mind. She didn't want that thought to be there. She tried to shake it off, but it was the last image that she had of Jessi. She tried to think about the good times together. She thought about when the two of them were in second grade, and they were the class winners at Foursquare, and how happy they were. They had a party to celebrate. She thought about the party, but then the image of Jessi's lifeless body overshadowed everything. She closed her eyes and shook her head, collapsing to the ground and wiping away the endless tears that escaped her eyes. Then she heard a radio strapped to the belt of one of the paramedics, and what she heard sent her emotions spiraling downward again.

"County General. We're pulling into the ER entrance. Notify the cardiologist on call. The patient coded but we were able to resuscitate after sixty seconds."

Erin went numb.

# CHAPTER 4

## GRANDMA

Somehow, Erin heard her name being called through the sounds of cars, chatter, crying, and reunions. She turned to see her mother running toward her. Erin stood on wobbly legs and ran to meet her. They hugged, and Erin cried harder. She was happy to see her mother and was suddenly grateful to be alive, and the tears that ran down her face were tears of joy. She also shed tears of fear and worry about Jessi.

"It's alright, sweetheart," her mother said, comforting her. She held her at arm's length, looking her up and down. "Are you hurt?" she asked.

"Just shaken up, Mom," Erin said. "But Jessi…" Erin swallowed hard and felt more tears filling her eyes.

"What is it?"

"I heard the ambulance driver say Jessi's heart stopped. She was bleeding, and she wouldn't open her eyes."

Erin's mom hugged her. "I'm sure she'll be fine. Let's get you home once the paramedics have cleared you."

"No!" Erin said, pulling away from her mother. "Can we please go to the hospital? I want to make sure Jessi is okay."

Erin's mom nodded as another paramedic approached the small group to Erin a final check.

At the hospital, Jessi was wheeled into the Emergency Room where a cardiac team was waiting. She was hooked up to numerous medical devices, including a heart monitor, which raced wildly as her heart beat out of control and, from time to time, stopped completely. The doctors worked feverishly to restart her heart, and they succeeded each time. But every time it stopped, it seemed to stop for a longer period of time. The doctors worried about how long her heart would stop and hoped CPR would prevent brain death.

Jessi watched from the top of the room. She could see and hear everything happening but did so helplessly. "I don't want to die," she said. "I have too much to do. Too much and too many people to live for!"

"We never feel the time is right, Jessi," a voice said, "but sometimes it's just our time."

Jessi turned to see her grandmother next to her. Somehow, she wasn't surprised. "But I don't feel it's time yet. It can't be!"

The Chief Cardiologist looked down at Jessi's body and then over at the heart monitor, which wailed its mono-toned sound, indicating no heartbeat or life.

"I'm going to call it," the Doctor said.

Grandma Vicci looked at Jessi and said, "It might not be time. And perhaps you'll go back. However, be aware that if you do, your world will change in ways you can't imagine."

"I'm willing to accept that, Grandma," Jessi said.

"Then back you must go, my grandchild."

And with that, Jessi felt herself take a deep, sharp breath and open her eyes. The heart monitor broke the silence with the rhythmic sound of a solid and healthy heartbeat.

Every medical person in the room stared momentarily and then sprang into action, gathering around Jessi and taking vital signs.

Jessi tried to brush them away. "Please stop. I'm fine. I just want to see my parents."

"Jessi," the Doctor said, gently easing her back on the bed, "you gave us all a huge scare. We'd love for you to give us a little time to check you out and make sure that we can verify how you say you're feeling."

Jessi gave a big sigh. "When can I see my parents?"

"I don't think they're here yet," the Doctor said, placing a stethoscope on Jessi's chest, "but I'll make sure someone notifies them."

"Thank you," Jessi said and took another deep breath.

The O'Donnells pulled into the hospital parking lot. They hurried to the Emergency Room entrance, where the guard at the door held up his hand and instructed them to empty their pockets into the tray and walk through the metal detector.

"We're not here for ourselves," Mrs. O'Donnell said in a panicked voice, "we're here for our daughter. She was in an accident!"

"I'll get you both through quickly," the guard said and hurried them through the metal detector. He escorted them to the desk.

The nurse behind the desk looked up with a smile. "How can I help you today?"

They asked about their daughter. "Her name is Jessie. Jessi O'Donnell. We received a call that she was here, and the Doctor asked us to come immediately. Is she okay?"

"Yes," the nurse said, "she's back in room five. I'll have someone take you back there."

They thanked the guard who stood patiently waiting. He nodded politely and said, "I hope your daughter is okay."

Another nurse appeared and escorted them back to the curtained-off area. When they pushed through, expecting the worse. They saw their daughter sitting on the end of the bed while the Doctor looked into her eyes with a small flashlight.

Mrs. O'Donnell gasped when she saw the butterfly stitch on Jessi's head and some dried blood that hadn't been cleaned off her face.

The Doctor looked over when he heard them enter. "Oh, hello," she said, holding out her hand. "I'm Doctor Lambert. You must be Jessi's parents."

The couple nodded. Dad shook the Doctor's hand, and Mom ran to be with her daughter. She hugged her and didn't want to ever let go. Jessi, being a teenager, was ready to shrug off everything, but with the events of the day, she returned the hug with the same intensity as her mother.

Mr. O'Donnell asked the Doctor, "How is she? We heard that she was unconscious in the accident. Anything we should know about?"

"Actually," the Doctor said nonchalantly, "she was a little worse than that. When the paramedics got her into the ambulance, she wasn't breathing. She had quite the bump on the head. But, the paramedics in the ambulance did a great job bringing her back."

"Bringing her back?" her mother's eyes were wide as saucers. She released her hold on her daughter and stepped toward the Doctor. " What do you mean back? Back from where?"

"Back from not breathing," the Doctor said. "Mrs. O'Donnell, your daughter was in a serious accident and stopped breathing. Actually, the paramedics brought her back to life. Her heart had stopped in the ambulance, but only briefly before the medics got it going again, but then it stopped for a longer period once she was here." The Doctor looked at Jessi and then back to her parents. "We thought we would lose her, but she's a fighter and seems perfectly fine now. I don't know why these events happened, but she's here now and seems perfectly healthy."

"Her heart stopped?" her mother said. "Her *heart stopped several times*, and you thought you would *lose her*?" Her voice was rising to a level of anger. "You're saying our daughter died and acting like this happens daily. How can you just stand there and act like this was normal?"

"The human body is an interesting organism, Mrs. O'Donnell," the Doctor said, unmoved by her outburst. "Many times, we have problems when breathing stops from head trauma, and we become especially concerned when the heart stops. But your Jessi here, well, she's tough. She started breathing on her own once her heart was beating again in the ambulance, and once she was here she had some issues with her heart and her breathing. But it just got better and I can't explain it. She was alert, talkative, and asking about you and her friend, Erin and the two of you of course." The Doctor turned to walk back to her patient, "Except for that nasty bump and gash on her head, it was almost like nothing had happened. So we cleaned out the cut, checked her out thoroughly, gave her a tetanus shot, and she's almost good to go. I just need to finish a few routine tests."

The Doctor moved the flashlight across her eyes again and asked, "How are you feeling now, Jessi?"

"I feel fine except for a little throbbing in my head," she replied.

"Are you sure?" the Doctor asked.

Jessi sensed something was happening that the Doctor was concerned about, but she wanted to hear it from her. Just as she was about to ask, her mother stepped in.

"What do you mean?" Mrs. O'Donnell demanded. "Is there something else that we should be aware of?"

"In the ambulance, they hooked her up to get an EEG to look at her brainwaves. I looked at the strip and thought it looked a little off. So I showed it to our resident neurologist. He said that although he had never

18

seen anything like this small anomaly, he didn't think it was anything to worry about." The Doctor looked at Jessi and shook her head. "I don't know what to think. She seems fine now. I will prescribe rest and lots of it for a few days. Then, we'll see how she's doing and possibly have her back for a CT scan or an MRI if we have concerns."

"I'll make sure she rests," her mother said. "In the meantime, how much longer will she need to be in the hospital?"

"She's doing remarkably well," the Doctor said. "I want to run one or two more tests and ensure that she's really going to be okay, and we'll see. If she continues to show no signs of trauma, we'll send her home, but honestly, I'd like to keep her overnight just for observation. Then if she does well, we'll kick her out in the morning right after breakfast."

"I'd like to go home now if that's okay," Jessi said.

"Let the doctor decide when it's okay to go home, sweetheart," her mom said.

"Okay. Yeah, I guess so," Jessi sighed. "How is everyone else? Can I have my phone to talk to my friends and see if everyone else is okay?"

"Let's get you into a room," the Doctor said while typing her notes into the computer. Then we can get you your phone, bring up your clothes, and maybe even some lunch if you're hungry."

"Starving!" she said.

"Okay then," the Doctor said and laughed, "I'll start getting things set up." The Doctor disappeared through the curtain.

"We were very worried," her father said, walking over and putting his arm around his daughter.

"How is everyone else?" she asked again. "Erin was sitting right next to me. Was she okay? Do you know?"

"We spoke with her at the accident, and she had a few bumps but was mostly fine. She was a little shaken up, of course. I think that everyone was, but she was more worried about you. Did you know you were the only one taken to the hospital," her mother said.

"No, I didn't know that. Wow. That's awkward."

"Honey," her dad said, giving her a light hug, "your mom and I are going to run home. Grab your phone charger and a change of clothes. We also promised Erin we would let her know how you were doing. I'm sure she'll come by to visit later. Is there anything else you need from the house?"

"I don't think so, but thanks, Dad. I'll see you guys later." Jessi didn't know what all the fuss was about. Her heart had stopped, but it was going now. She felt good. In fact, she felt better than she had in a long time. She chalked it up to having a little nap on the way to the hospital. She had trouble believing that her heart had stopped at all. It didn't seem real.

Jessi spent the rest of the day in the hospital. Several of her friends came and went, and they exchanged stories about the accident. Erin stopped by in the afternoon with some flowers. She still felt the trauma of the morning's events, and tears came quickly. She expressed her concern about almost losing her friend and her joy that she didn't. They had a feeling that they'd be friends for life.

"I was so scared, Jess," Erin said, sitting by the side of the bed.

"Don't be scared anymore, silly," Jessi said. "I'm fine."

"But I just can't get the image of you all slumped over with the blood on your head."

Jessi became stern. "Look at me. Do you see any blood on my head?"

Erin looked at her friend, "No."

"Then stop worrying, silly. The only thing wrong with me is this stupid headache." Jessi winced and touched her temple.

"Do you need me to call the nurse?" Erin asked.

"No," Jessi said and smiled. "I'll be fine. I just need some rest."

Erin stood up and put her hand on Jessi's. "I'll let you get some rest. I'll come back with your parents tomorrow."

The two friends hugged, and Erin slowly made her way out of the hospital room. Jessi laid back and closed her eyes. She could hear people running by her room door and thought she could hear doctors yelling and doors slamming, but it almost echoed. It was as if the sounds were there, but they weren't there. She pressed the call button and was surprised when the nurse came in immediately.

"What can I get you, Jess?" the nurse asked.

"Could I get something for my headache, please?" she asked.

"Of course," the nurse said and turned to get the medication.

"Oh, and what's going on?" Jessi asked. "Out in the hall, I mean."

The nurse turned around and said, "Nothing. It's pretty quiet today. Why do you ask?"

"Oh, nothing," Jessi said, somewhat confused. "I must have fallen asleep. I thought that I heard people running by and others yelling."

The nurse laughed. "When we fall into a light sleep, sounds can become magnified, and things are exaggerated. Everything's fine. I'll get something for your head and be right back." The nurse smiled and left the room. Jessi closed her eyes and wondered.

Although she enjoyed being pampered by the hospital staff, Jessi was happy when the following day arrived, breakfast was over, and she could leave. Her mom came in, signed the paperwork, and walked alongside her daughter as she was wheeled to the front door by the orderly. "Here you go," the young man said. "Take care of yourself."

"Thank you," Jessi said and stood up. She walked to the waiting car and climbed in the back seat. Her mom thanked the young man again and got into the car.

As the car pulled out of the parking lot, Jessi looked back at the hospital and silently wished it goodbye but still wondered about the commotion she thought she heard the day before.

# CHAPTER 5

## SOUNDS

Over the next few days, Jessi's mother kept her home from school, insisting she should rest. But Jessi was a teenager and full of energy. She tried her best to be patient, but eventually, she couldn't take it anymore and insisted on returning to school.

Her mother reluctantly agreed, saying there were only a few days of school left in the week anyway, but told her, "If you feel the slightest bit of fatigue or dizziness, you make sure you call me, and I'll come to get you."

"Yes, Mother," Jessi sighed and hurried out the door.

She felt like a prisoner who had just been released from jail. She danced in the sunshine and skipped all the way to school. She looked at the flowers along the way, breathed in the fresh air, and enjoyed this part of life.

At school, her friends and teachers treated her like a celebrity and asked question after question. When she walked into class, the other students would cheer and clap. There was a mixture of curiosity and concern. She suddenly became the most popular person in the twelfth grade. Even the popular kids were envious of her, although they all admitted that they wouldn't want to go through what she had to gain that popularity.

"Hey Jessi," one student she didn't know raised his hand in Geometry class and asked, "what's it like to die? Did you see heaven? Did you see any famous people? Was Elvis there?" Everyone in the room laughed, and the teacher had to tell everyone to get back to work, although secretly, even the teachers wondered the same things.

Jessi became known as the girl who had died and came back.

Every "What was it like to die," question was met with her now standard answer, "I can't really remember much about it."

Sadly, that answer was neither flashy nor satisfying for those who asked. Being somewhat disappointed, they would smile and walk away.

As with all things, however, her popularity faded. Jessi returned to just being her, with an exciting past but a mundane present and uncertain future.

On this particular day, about two weeks from the day she was allowed to go back to school by her mother, Jessi was walking home. She had walked this route for years. Four years at the very least. But the point is, she knew the route very well and could walk it with her eyes closed. She had been born in this town, lived in the same house all her life, and knew every step between her house and the school. She knew the traffic and how it ran during the hours after school was out.

She approached the busy intersection with her usual caution. She looked up and down the street even after the light told her it was okay and safe to cross. It was a much quieter traffic day than usual, so it took her by great surprise when she walked a few yards after she had crossed the street and heard the screeching of tires sliding across the asphalt. Even worse, it was followed by a crash with metal twisting and glass shattering. The entire event made her jump! She turned around, expecting to see a terrible accident. It took a few seconds for her brain to comprehend what she saw. "What is going on?" She said to herself.

She saw nothing but a clear intersection. She ran back to the corner and looked up and down the street but still saw nothing unusual. She shook her head. *I hope I'm not going crazy,* she thought to herself. She took another look, turned, and cautiously walked home.

When she arrived home, she had all but forgotten the strange event. Tomorrow was Saturday, and she had a fantastic weekend planned. A day filled with movies and friends. Her head was abuzz with plans and things she needed to do.

"You should probably think about going to bed soon," her mother said.

"Believe me," she replied, "I've thought about that, but I am so excited about tomorrow that I'm not sure I'll get to sleep at all tonight."

Her mother took her by the shoulders, turned her around, and moved her toward the stairs. "Give it a try," she said, nudging Jessi.

"Fine," Jessi said. "Goodnight, Mom."

"Goodnight, sweetheart!"

The next day was beautiful. Better than Jessi had hoped for. She, Erin, and a few other friends went to the movies and had their fill of popcorn, pop, and fun. They walked out and stood at the edge of the sidewalk.

"What should we do now?" Erin said.

"Mall?" Jessi asked and looked around.

"The mall sounds perfect," Nancy, another friend, said.

"All in favor?" Erin said, raising her hand.

"Aye!" Everyone shouted and laughed.

"Beat you there," Jessi called out and took off running. The other girls ran after her.

"I wiin!" Jessi said, touching the entrance door and out of breath.

The other girls huffed and puffed.

Erin grabbed the other door handle and yelled, "Beat you inside!" She ran in followed by the others, all laughing.

The girls walked from store to store, looking at fashions, shoes, and jeans and spraying each other with perfume samples.

"Graduation is coming soon," Erin said. "Have you all thought about colleges?"

"I'm taking a year off," Nancy said.

"What will you do for that year," Jessi asked.

"Work. Save money. Apply to schools." She said. "Not sure which ones, though. How about you?"

"I'm heading off down the road to the State College. I want to study accounting, business, or even real estate. I'd like to become an appraiser."

"Hey," Erin said, pouting, "that's what I was going to do. Copy cat."

"I'm pretty sure you are copying me, girl. We haven't even discussed it until now."

All three girls laughed.

By the time Jessi returned home, she was happily exhausted. She walked in and immediately heard her mother in the kitchen.

"Mom! I'm home!" Jessi yelled. She walked in and sat at the dining room table with a thump. Spreading her arms, she tilted her head back. "I love life!" She said.

"That's good," her mother said flatly.

"Are you okay, mom?"

"Yeah."

"What's wrong?"

Her mom turned from the stove. "Jessi, I worry about you."

"I know you do, Mom, but you don't have to."

"Do you think it's a choice?" Her mom walked over and sat at the table.

"Jessi, I love you. You're my child. No matter how old you get, you'll always be my child. I almost lost you in an accident. Now I can't get that out of my head."

"But I'm here now," Jessi said. "I know you worry. You balance out Dad. I don't think he ever worries."

"Oh, he does. He just doesn't show it as much. We both worry."

Jessi reached over and took her mother's hand. "Try not to worry. I'm not planning on going anywhere, and if you keep worrying, you'll never be able to enjoy the person I'm growing into."

Jessi's mom nodded, and Jessi stood from her seat, walked over and and gave her a hug. "Teach me what you're cooking!"

Jessi's mom laughed. "I'm making burgers."

"Teach me how to make mom's famous burgers, then," Jessi said, pulling her mom from the chair. They both laughed, hugged, and made the best burgers ever made!

The following day, Jessi woke up early. Her mom was making breakfast, and her dad was still in bed. "He had a busy week," her mom explained, "and he had to work overtime yesterday, so I thought it would be nice to let him sleep in a little today. I'm making pancakes. I know how much you like them. Why don't you go out and grab the paper before we sit down and eat."

Jessi went outside to get the Sunday paper. She enjoyed looking through the weekly store ads and was happy that her parents didn't follow the trend of many others who had canceled their subscriptions. Because it was a heavier paper today, it didn't quite make it to the porch, so she scurried down the walkway and picked it up. The heading of the front-page story caught her eye, and she opened the paper to read it while slowly walking back to the door. As she perused the story, she stopped to read the first few paragraphs repeatedly. She felt light-headed, and her knees felt weak, but she was able to make her way back into the house. When she got inside, her dad was sitting at the table. Jessi stood silently, trying to comprehend what she had read.

"Good morning, sweetheart!" he said to her. "I was starting to think that you got lost out there."

Without saying a word, Jessi handed the paper to her father and plopped down in a chair at the table. She stared at the table while her father started looking at the headlines.

"Thanks, sweetheart," he said to her.

"Um, yeah, no problem." Jessi sat silently, thinking about what she had read, waiting for her dad to say aloud what she already knew.

Her dad let out a whistle. "There's all sorts of news today," he started. "Looks like there's a burglar on the loose. Guess we start locking the doors again and arming the house alarm at night." He looked at Jessi. "You need to be extra careful at night. No more sneaking out."

"I don't sneak out at night, Dad," she said indignantly.

Jessi's mom gave her a look. It was the look moms give when they know something but won't say it.

"Okay, not as often as I used to." Jessi went back to looking distracted, waiting for her father to progress through the daily news.

"Holy cow!" he exclaimed. "There was a huge accident at Shields and Drake yesterday. Three people were killed, and two others are in critical condition at the hospital. I'm surprised we didn't hear that. It's just up the road. Did either of you hear anything yesterday?"

"I remembered hearing some sirens yesterday, but I hear them around here so often anymore that I didn't think anything of it, really," Jessi's mom said as she brought a plate of pancakes to the table. "The bacon will be ready shortly."

Jessi sat quietly and tried not to think about what her brain was forcing her to re-live.

"I can't believe it was that bad," her mom continued. Are there any names? Anyone we know?"

"The names haven't been released yet, pending notification of the families. Tragic, though." Jessi's dad shook his head.

Jessi's mom had put the bacon on a platter and brought it to the table when she noticed that Jessi looked a little pale and hadn't attacked the stack of pancakes as usual. She nudged her husband, who also looked over at his daughter.

"You okay, sweetheart?" he asked.

Jessi's mind was whirling out of control. She heard the sounds in her head repeatedly, trying to make sense of it all. She was so absorbed in thought that she didn't hear her father's question.

"Jessi!" Her mother said louder.

Jessi jumped at the sound of her name and looked up. Her dad and mom were looking at her. Mom was concerned, and Dad smiled, although the smile was weak.

"What? I'm okay," Jessi said. "Just thinking about the accident. Horrible thing. I can't even imagine." Her voice trailed off as she spoke the words.

"Do you know who was involved?" her mother asked. "Did you hear something about it from your friends? I know how fast news travels these days with all of your texting and such."

"Hear something?" Jessi said. "Um, well, it's just that…"

"Honey, what is it?" her mom asked, sitting at the table.

"Um, now please don't think this is weird or anything, and mom, don't get all upset, but, well, it's just that, I heard the accident happen the day before it happened."

"Maybe you just had a premonition or something. You know, your Aunt Betty used to have those. Only hers came as dreams at night. It was eerie how accurate they were sometimes. Maybe that's it. Maybe you dreamt it." Her mom was trying hard to play it off.

"No, that's not it at all, and I'm serious Mom," Jessi said. "It wasn't a dream, and it wasn't at night. Dad, did you say it happened yesterday afternoon, around three-thirty?"

"I don't think I said," her father replied. He scanned the story. "Yeah, here it is. The accident happened at three-thirty-two."

Jessi's stomach twisted into knots. "When I was walking home from school on Friday, I crossed that intersection, and right after I got to the other side of the street, I heard a huge crash. It scared me, but when I looked, there was nothing there. Not a single car. It sounded real like it was really happening. Then I heard sirens, and then, nothing. The sirens faded away. It was like a dream, but I was wide awake, Mom. Then the next day, it really happened."

Jessi's parents stared at her, not knowing what to say. Her dad opened his mouth and then closed it again. He looked at his wife, who was also at a loss for words. They both looked back at their daughter.

"What?" she asked.

"Um," her dad started. "You must admit that your story sounds a little out of the ordinary."

"Crazy?" Jessi asked.

"No. Just unusual," Jessi's dad responded calmly.

Jessi's mom asked questions the rest of the day but didn't get the answers she wanted. Not because Jessi was stubborn but because she didn't understand it herself. Her mom thought it had to do with her recent head injury, but just to be sure, she suggested they set up an appointment with an audiologist.

"My hearing is fine, Mom," Jessi would say.

"You heard something that wasn't there," her mom said.

"I heard something that wasn't there yet," Jessi said.

"It wasn't there, Jess," her mom said again. "It wasn't there at all."

"Until the next day!" Jessi said, frustrated at the conversation.

"It hadn't happened yet, Jessica."

Jessi pursed her lips and decided to stop talking. She knew that when her mom used her formal name, she wouldn't let up on this. She didn't understand what Jessi was trying to say, and nothing would change that.

So her mom insisted that she have her hearing tested, and that was the end of the conversation.

Jessi hoped that her mom would just forget about it, but later that week, Jessi found herself sitting in the audiologist's office after a long and silent drive.

Jessi had objected several times, going to the doctor's against her will but was overruled at each turn by her mother. Jessi was convinced that it was a waste of time. She knew what she had heard. Also that her hearing was as good or better than ever. Why her mother insisted on wasting her money on these tests was beyond her, but there was nothing she could say or do to change her mother's mind, so she just waited silently and fumed.

When the nurse came out and called Jessi back, her mom followed.

"You don't have to go with me, Mom. I'm a big girl now."

"I'm going with you to see what the doctor says, nothing more."

Jessi was placed in a soundproof booth. At first, she imagined that she was a singer about to record a song, but when the doctor brought out the most oversized and unflattering set of headphones she had ever seen, the fantasy quickly disappeared.

"I need you to put these on," the doctor said flatly. "I'm going to go out in the other room. We'll be able to see each other through the glass window there," the doctor pointed to the obvious pane of glass in front of Jessi, "and I'll initiate a series of sounds. If and when you hear a sound, I want you to raise your hand on the side that you hear the sound. For example, raise your left hand if you hear a sound in the left ear. If you hear the sound in both ears, raise both hands. Simple enough. Go ahead and put on the headphones, and we'll get started. Any questions?"

Jessi thought about asking if he really got paid for doing this but thought better of it. Instead, she just shook her head and put on the headphones. The doctor left and sat at the control panel. Her mother sat behind him, smiled, and waved. Jessi smiled back weakly.

She sat in the room listening to the annoying tones of varying frequencies and volumes. She would raise one hand or the other and occasionally shoot a dirty look at her mom sitting outside the booth. Her mom looked casual but at the same time concerned. She would glance over at the readings and then back at Jessi, offering her a flat smile. Her mom had no idea what the readings meant, nor did she know what normal was. Jessi could tell that her mom wanted desperately to ask questions but practiced restraint.

After what seemed like hours, but in reality, was only a few minutes, the doctor finally came back into the booth.

"All done," he said, lifting the headphones off Jessi's head. "Let's head to my office to talk about what you heard!"

He led Jessi and her mom into his office, where the two women sat on one side of a desk across from the doctor, who sat in a plush chair on the business side of the desk.

The doctor spoke to Jessi's mom mostly but looked at Jessi from time to time. "Your daughter seems to have normal hearing," he said, looking at the results on his computer. "In fact, she hears better than many girls her age. I assume you don't blast music from your phone or Ear Pods?"

Jessi shook her head. "I don't need to. I enjoy music for the music. "I don't have to turn it way up to get into it."

Mrs. O'Donnell spoke up. "Well, thank you, doctor," she said. "We appreciate you checking her."

Jessi and her mom stood up, and Jessi started toward the door. Her mom, however, lingered behind for a moment.

"Uh, doctor," she started, glancing over at Jessi.

"Yes?"

Jessi's mom lowered her voice to a whisper. "When you were checking her, did she happen to hear anything at the wrong time? Did she indicate that she was hearing a sound when there was no sound?"

"I don't understand," the doctor said.

Jessi stopped at the door and turned around. "Are you coming?"

"I'll be right there, sweetheart. How about I just meet you at the car," she said nervously.

Jessi started back over to the two people conversing while her mom, not seeing Jessi's advance, whispered again, "Did she hear anything or any sounds when there weren't any?"

"MOM!" Jessi shouted. "I can't believe you asked him that! He told you that I hear better than most teenagers. Why can't you just leave it at that? I hear what I hear. Maybe you don't understand it or just think I'm crazy, but I'll answer for the doctor and say, no, I didn't hear anything when there wasn't something there. I'll wait for you outside." She turned toward the door, embarrassed, and stormed out of the office.

The confused doctor looked at Jessi's mom and said, "Mrs. O'Donnell, your daughter's hearing was perfect, as I said, much better than many girls her age. I don't understand your question, and it appears your daughter doesn't understand why you asked it either."

"Well, never mind. I'm just being a neurotic mom. Thank you very much, doctor." Mrs. O'Donnell quickly left the office to catch up with her daughter.

Jessi stood by the locked car, her arms folded and leaning against the door. Her mom reached the car and unlocked the doors. Jessi got in and slammed her door. Her mom got into the driver's seat, started the car, and began to drive.

The silence was intense. Jessi stared out of her window, not acknowledging her mother. Her mother decided to break the silence.

"I know you're upset with me, sweetheart. I'm sorry if I embarrassed you at the doctor's office. Please understand that I'm just being a concerned mom. Neither of us understands what's happening and why you heard what you heard."

Jessi could feel her anger coming to a boil. It reached a point where she could no longer hold it in. "Why did you have to do that? Why? Even after the doctor said, there was nothing wrong. Don't you think he's professional enough that he would have said something if I had been pointing at the stars when there was no sound? I've been telling you that it was probably a coincidence that I heard something. But I did hear it. I honest to God I did hear it. It made me jump. It startled me. I went back to see if it was out of my sight. I heard it! I'm not going to say I didn't, and Mom, you have to believe me when I say that there's nothing wrong with me! I just can't explain it."

"It's just that I'm worried about you, Jess," her mom said. "You can't be mad at me for worrying about you. You can't blame me for worrying about what happened to you, wanting you to be healthy, and loving you as a parent."

Jessi felt her feelings melting, and a small smile started slipping across her lips. "No," she said, "I guess. But," she turned to her mom and said sternly, "don't ever embarrass me like that again. Ever! What you said was just crazy, and I don't want anybody to think I'm crazy. I'm not, you know. I'm as sane as you and Dad, maybe even more sane. I've seen the two of you and how you act sometimes." Jessi noticed that her mother was beginning to cry. A small tear rolled down her face, and her chin quivered. As her eyes filled with tears and her vision blurred, she pulled the car to the side of the road. Putting the car in park, she sat quietly while the tears rolled down her face. She hated crying when she had to talk. It seemed like every word about why she was crying made the tears fall faster and the words more difficult to say.

She finally forced a sentence, "I just want you to be okay, sweetheart." Just saying that much sent Jessi's mother into a sobbing fit. She put her face in her hands and continued to sob while Jessi leaned over and put her hand on her mother's shoulder.

"Don't cry, Mom," she said. "It's okay, and I'm going to be fine. I'll never bring it up again."

Her mom looked at her. "No, no. I don't want you to hide things from me, either. I just want you to be okay. I want you to be healthy. I worry about what happened to you on the bus and in the ambulance. It hurts my heart to think about the fact that you almost...."

Jessi waited for the word that didn't come, so she said it. "Died?"

"Yes! Yes, you died. You died, and your father and I almost lost you. What if you hadn't come back? What if we had lost you? What if these things you heard means something is wrong with your brain? I couldn't stand it if anything happened to you, sweetheart.

"I understand, Mom, but you must understand I'm alive and fine. We can't concentrate on the 'what ifs' in life. I can tell you this, though, if I had died and not returned, I'd be haunting you and Dad for a long time. At least now, I'll probably move out someday and give you guys some freedom. Well, maybe."

Her mom stared at her for a moment. Jessi looked dead serious. She suddenly realized what she had said. "Dead" serious. She smiled. The smile turned into a laugh. Jessi laughed with her. She dried her eyes and hugged her daughter. "How did you grow up so fast and become so wise?"

"Who knows," Jessi said. "It just happened."

Jessi's mom pulled back out into traffic and headed toward the house. On the way, Jessi vowed to herself that she would never tell anyone about the sounds again, if she continued to hear them. As she thought that, she heard a fire truck siren pass them. She tried not to react but turned to look anyway. When she didn't see anything, she turned back in her seat.

"Did you see somewhere you wanted me to stop?" her mom asked.

"Yeah," Jessi replied. "Let's stop for an ice cream cone. Is that okay?"

Her mom smiled and turned the car around to head toward the nearest ice cream shop.

# CHAPTER 6

## FUTURE

Despite her vow to never reveal her ability to hear future sounds, Jessi had already told her best friend, Erin. Erin thought it was cool and wished that she could do it.

"Have you heard anything today?" Erin would ask.

"Not today," Jessi would say in a low voice.

"Let me know if you do," Erin would whisper back.

Then Jessi would put her hand on her forehead, close her eyes and say, "I hear someone being strangled to death in this very spot for asking too many questions!"

"Ha, ha. Very funny."

"I don't hear every sound that happens in the future," Jessi said to Erin as they were walking home after school. "I hear couples arguing, parents scolding their children, accidents and the occasional phantom siren speeding down the street. I can hear students threatening or fighting. Sometimes I can hear crying and something being said about grades. Nothing too exciting."

"What do you mean? It's all exciting," Erin said. Then she would question Jessi endlessly about who it could be and why they were so upset about whatever it was. She asked Jessi if she thought she could stop whatever she heard happen, from happening.

"I'm not sure," Jessi said thoughtfully. I don't really remember returning to a specific location to actually see the event, although sometimes I've walked by someplace accidentally and the event was already playing out."

This whole thing changed Jessi. Where before she was outgoing and made friends easily, she now shied away from making new friends and drifted away from old ones. It was easier to keep things to herself than it was to explain sudden moments of surprise at nothing. Only Erin remained her confidant and understanding friend. In high school, friendships come and go, so not many of her old friends pursued the drifting relationships.


Before long, high school ended and Jessi walked with her friends to receive her diploma. Her mother cried and her father beamed.

During the summer, she worked to earn money to help with college. After the summer ended, she went to the local college and stayed in the dorms for her first year. Erin was right there and they became dorm mates.

When she left, her mother cried and her father was sad. "You can come home anytime you need anything, even if it's just for a home cooked meal," her mother told her. Jessi smiled and took her up on the offer, frequently during her first year, and then less over the next three years. As she settled into her new routine of independence, the visits turned into phone calls from her, then phone calls from her parents and eventually slowed to holidays and special occasions.

During her college days, Jessi found that her ability to hear the future came in handy when dating. She also found out that she could at least influence the outcome of some of the things she heard. If a guy was going to break-up with her, she could hear, in her ear, the phone call. The next day, she would be proactive and call him first, telling him to get lost. She knew what he was going to say anyway and how he would say it, so it gave her great satisfaction to be the one breaking up and not the one being dumped.

By her third year in college, Jessi had found an apartment and lived by herself. When she graduated, she found a job, locally, with Thompson Appraisals. Erin was right there by her side and was also welcomed into the Thompson family.

The two had been working for about a year, appraising properties and helping the business to grow. Jessi had progressed faster than Erin but still asked her to help with assignments that she had to go on. On this particular day, Erin and Jessi walked down the hallway, talking about the day on their way toward the front door.

"I can't believe that guy thought his building was worth a million," she said to Erin, chuckling.

34

"I think that was the most poorly maintained building I've seen in this town. It might have been worth a lot more if he had taken care of it," Erin replied. "But the way he neglected it, he'll be lucky to get a hundred thousand for it, and that would be for the land only. Did you see the water damage?"

"Yeah," Jessi said, "it's amazing how people don't think about the future of their assets because they think they're saving a few bucks."

"I can't believe the things you caught," Erin said. "I never would have thought of looking in some of the places you looked."

"You'll get there," Jessi said. "It just takes time."

"Yeah, but I've driven by the building a million times," Erin said, "and it looked fine to me. Now I'm surprised that no one had condemned it!"

They continued to walk down the hall laughing. As they approach the cubical area, Erin nudged Jessi and pointed to a particular desk. Sitting at the desk was an old friend from high school, Jim Johnson. Jim wasn't an extraordinarily good-looking man. He was around the same age as Jessi and Erin and went to the same schools. He had dark hair and was on the thin side. His clothes weren't the latest fashion and tended to be well worn. When he heard the laughter, he looked up from his work and suddenly became lost in the vision. He had always had a crush on Jessi, ever since middle school, but he was too shy to say anything to her. Now, here he was, a working man, and he still couldn't get the nerve to talk to the woman of his dreams. He imagined, however, that he could jump up out of his chair and run over to her, acting very suave and sophisticated, and sweep her off of her feet. She would smile and compliment him and agree to go out with him. Sitting at his desk, he smiled slightly at the thought and then realized that the two women were looking back at him. Suddenly flustered, he looked away, embarrassed to be caught staring and in the daydream, wondering if either of them knew what he was thinking. He tried being casual, but turned and knocked over a pencil holder on his desk. As he tried to grab for the falling container, he accidentally overcorrected and knocked the container again, sending the pencils flying and eliciting moans from his surrounding co-workers.

"I think he likes you," Erin chided.

"Maybe he likes *you*!" Jessi returned the chiding.

"Whatever!" she replied. "Keep dreaming."

Jessi had always noticed Jim in school and thought that he was a nice boy. She had entertained the thought of possibly hanging out with him, but it was always a short-lived thought.

The two women continued on. Jessi stopped by her office to drop off a few supplies and then headed to the door out of the building with Erin by her side. It had been a long day and Jessi was ready to go have some fun girl time with her friend.

When they reached the parking lot, Jessi looked over at her car and noticed four guys, who also worked for the company, hovering around and near her car. They were whispering and looking in the direction of the girls. She slowed down and leaned toward Erin.

"What do you think this is all about?" she asked.

"I don't know," Erin replied, "but maybe if we ignore them they'll go away."

As they approached Jessi's car, the men pointed and stood up straight, clearing their throats. One man, who was more toward the front of her car, stepped up, blocking Jessi's way. He sidestepped as Jessi tried to go around, continuing to block her path.

"Hey Jessi," the man said, "heard any good jokes lately?"

"No, now excuse me. I've had a long day and want to get home."

"Oh, I'm so sorry, but are you sure you haven't heard any good jokes lately? Like maybe something that we'll be telling tomorrow?"

The other men sputtered laughs.

Erin stepped up. "Bug off creep."

The man looked Erin up and down and said, "So what special and magical powers do *you* have?"

"I have the power to make jerks, like you, shrivel up into toads and die in the hot sun, or just die, by looking at them. It depends on my mood and what is more amusing to me at the time." Erin didn't blink and only smiled an evil smile. She started to raise her hands as if to cast an evil spell.

At first, the men weren't sure what to think and took a small step back. The man blocking their way stepped back up and was angry.

"Think you're pretty hot, don't you? Well, you've got another thing coming if you think you can scare me. Maybe we should see how tough you really are," he said getting in her face.

Right about then another voice broke in from just behind Jessi and Erin. "What's going on here?" It was Jim, who was on his way to his car.

"Bug off, dweeb!" the man said. "This is none of your concern."

"Now hold on just a minute," Jim said taking a few steps toward him. "I don't want any trouble, John. I just wanted to talk to Jessi for a little bit. You don't mind, do you? Just a little talking?"

"No," John said. "I don't mind talking, if I'm doing the talking. But if you want to talk, maybe you'd like to talk to this." John stepped up and pushed Jim, hard. Jim stumbled back, losing his balance, and fell backward to the ground. One of John's friends walked over and put his foot on Jim's chest, holding him down.

Jessi had seen enough. It's one thing to try and intimidate her, but it's something completely different when a bully picks on someone who is helpless. She sauntered up to John. "You know," she purred, "I really, really like a man who is in charge and tough. A man who knows what he wants and isn't afraid to use force to get it. Are you that kind of man?"

"Oh, you know I am," he said suddenly changing his attitude and tone.

Jessi started to rub his chest, then reached down to take his hand. Once she had his hand, she turned it and applied a Kung Fu leverage to it, locking his wrist and dropping him to his knees.

John groaned in pain and yelled, "I give! I give! Stop! You're hurting me!"

"Am I?" Jessi cooed. "Oh, that disappoints me. A frail little girl is hurting you? I'm so sorry. I thought you were tougher than that."

With that, Jessi released her hold.

John slowly stood up, rubbing his wrist. Jessi shot a glance at the man whose foot was on Jim's chest. The man immediately removed his foot. Jessi smiled at him and asked. "Want to hold hands?"

The guy slowly shook his head and backed away from Jim.

Jessi turned her attention back to John. "Now, go away and don't bother us anymore! That's just a taste of what will happen if you ever try this kind of thing with us again."

John held his sore hand, but Jessi knew he wasn't hurt badly, and that the pain would be gone within ten minutes. "If you can hear the future," he growled at her, "then you'd better listen for me and watch your back. Nobody does this to me and gets away with it."

"Really?" Jessi said and stepped closer to a retreating John. "If you feel like you can threaten me and intimidate me, you had better think twice buddy boy. If I ever see you slinking around my car, my friends or anywhere, acting like you're going to hurt those people that I call friends and family, I'd suggest that you make sure your health insurance is all up to date and that you've met your deductible, because the damage I do to you will be far worse than just a little wrist lock pain, it will require several days in the hospital, and if you really make me mad, it would be several days in intensive care. Do you understand me?"

John was visibly shaken. No one had ever stood up to him like this and he didn't know how to react. He wanted to run, but he didn't want to lose face in front of his friends.

Jessi stomped her foot in a move toward John, which made him jump. He glared at Jessi and turned to his friends. "Come on. Let's get out of here."

The men started to back away. Erin stomped her foot toward them and hissed like an angry cat, causing them to scurry off and almost fall in the process.

"You're crazy!" John shouted. "You'll pay for this!"

The four men ran quickly away. Jessi and Erin giggled and then turned their attention toward Jim, who was still lying on the ground but attempting to get up. Both Erin and Jessi walked over and helped Jim to his feet. He brushed himself off and looked a little embarrassed.

"Thanks for trying to help, Jim," Jessi said. "That was very sweet of you to come to our rescue."

Jim smiled and blushed even more than he had been. "You were amazing!" he said. "It was like watching a Bruce Lee movie, only better!" Jim took the stance that the Karate Kid took at the end of his first movie. He let out a loud "Waaaaa!" and executed a very weak and uncoordinated double kick. Then he resumed a typical martial arts stance and started chopping through the air, wildly, with both hands as if attacking a mysterious and unseen opponent. Jessi and Erin laughed out loud at the sight until they couldn't take it anymore.

"Maybe we should teach you some real Kung Fu sometime," Erin said out of breath from the laughter.

"I don't know," Jessi joined in, "he might just end up hurting himself."

"No, no," Jim said. "I'd love to learn sometime. I wanted to take some classes when I was a kid, but my parents wouldn't let me."

"Really? Why was that?" Jessi asked.

Jim was quiet for a moment and, again, began to turn red. "Well, uh, they said, uh, that I might hurt myself."

The laughter resumed. Eventually, it slowed and there was an awkward silence. As they stood lost in the silence, not knowing what to say, Erin spoke up.

"Jess," she said, "I need to get going. I'm supposed to meet Barry for dinner tonight and I still have to go home and shower, and change and do my hair and so on."

"I totally understand," Jessi said. "Thanks for walking with me to the car. I always appreciate you. Go and get ready. Maybe you and I can hang out tomorrow night."

"I wish you would get a boyfriend so that we could double sometime. Not even a boyfriend, just a date!" Erin realized that the words probably shouldn't have come out in front of Jim, but it was too late to take them back. She glanced at Jim and saw the hopeful look on his face. She glanced back at Jessi and winked.

"Erin, you know how I feel about all of this. After, you know, what happened. Well, I just don't believe in love. I don't believe that anyone can love me unconditionally. I don't believe that anyone can accept me for who I am and what I can, or can't do. Look at you and Barry. You two are always fighting. He tries to change you and you try to change him and it doesn't go anywhere except in a big circle of grief. I say no thank you to that. If there is someone out there for me, then that's great. But I doubt that anyone will ever get the chance to show me. It would take a big event in my life for me to let anyone in. You're my friend, and I love that we're friends, and friendship is all I really need. So don't count on a double date anytime in the near future. But, thanks for being concerned. You really are a good friend!"

Jessi looked at Jim and said, "I need to get going too. It's been a long day. Thanks again, Jim, for helping out and coming to our rescue."

"I don't feel like I did much," he said modestly. "But, I'm glad I was a distraction."

Jessi unlocked the door to her car and reached for the door handle. "Hey, uh, Jessi?" Jim stammered. "Maybe we could get together sometime and, uh, you know, grab a coffee or something, sometime."

Jessi looked over at Erin who just smiled and shrugged as she climbed into her car. She mouthed the words, "Good luck" as she shut the door and started her car.

Jessi looked back at Jim. "Yeah," she smiled. "We'll have to see. Let's talk later and see what happens."

"Okay," Jim said beaming. "Sure! That sounds great! I'll see you tomorrow and maybe we can talk then."

"It's a date," Jessi said and then regretted using that phrase. "See you tomorrow, Jim."

Jessi climbed into her car, shut the door and started the engine. She gave Jim a final smile and wave and she drove off.

Jim watched her drive away, feeling great and almost skipping to his car. He was very happy with how the day turned out, feeling like he'd made some progress toward a new relationship. For the first time in years, he had been able to speak to the girl he thought about constantly and dreamed about often. He was ready to take that next big step and go out on a date with her. She didn't say yes, but most importantly, she didn't say no, and that's what he was afraid she *would* say. So, there was a chance, There was hope. Tomorrow would be a great day of accomplishment! He got into his car, still smiling, and drove away.

Across the parking lot, a man stood in the shadows of the oak trees and behind the chest-high bushes, watching the events that had just played out. He hit the nearby tree with his fist and mumbled something under his breath. He watched Jim drive away and clenched his fists, then turned and walked to a nearby car. He climbed in and slammed the door, started the car and peeled out of the parking lot.

# CHAPTER 7

## THREATS

The following day was typical. Jessi woke up, got ready, and headed to work. The morning was sunny and cool, with a brilliant blue sky overhead. Jessi loved mornings like this, and they made her feel like nothing could ever go wrong with the world.

She arrived at work and said hello to each person she passed. She didn't see John or his cohorts, but then she didn't ever go to the shipping dock where they worked, so she probably wouldn't see them. She wondered how they knew about her ability to hear the future. She knew Erin would never discuss that, especially with guys like those. She wondered who else knew.

She walked into her office and sat at her desk. She looked at the pile of papers that needed to be taken care of and sighed.

She finally got into a routine of doing paperwork and setting appointments. "I just can't figure out how Kohn and his buddies knew about how I hear the future," she said to herself. She heard someone walk by her door and realized she was talking aloud, so just thought. *Word gets around,* she thought. *Maybe they overheard Erin and I talking once. I need to be more careful about where I talk about it.* She shrugged to herself and continued with her regular morning routine.

Most days like today were slow and somewhat boring. She liked it that way. So she thought it was odd when her phone rang. She had always thought of her phone as more of a paperweight on her desk. If anyone wanted to communicate with her, they would Email and occasionally drop by her office or text. No one ever used the phone anymore. She picked up the receiver. "This is Jessi."

The voice on the other end of the phone was distorted and unrecognizable. It was much like those disguised voices you hear on television cop shows. She wondered who was pranking her when the voice said, "Yes. I know."

But the tone of the voice was serious, and she found it a little unsettling.

"Who's this?" she asked, expecting it to be someone from the next office.

"It's a beautiful day, don't you think?" the voice asked. "Too bad you're stuck inside. I know how much you enjoy the sunshine. Don't you hate it when you're inside a building and can't get out? I bet that enclosed places make you feel uncomfortable..."

Jessi hung up the phone. She was shaking. It was one thing to confront someone who wanted to hurt you. She was always able to handle that, but having someone speak to you over the phone and not know who that person was; that was not okay. This wasn't a prank. This was creepy and weird. She stared at the phone. *Who was that? What did they want? Why did they call?* She jumped when her boss knocked at her door.

"Hey Jessi, have you got a minute?" Gary Thompson was a man in his sixties. He was thin with gray hair but distinguished-looking. He had kind eyes. Jessi had noticed that the first time she saw him. He was also a great people person, and though he was not nosey, he wanted to make sure those who worked for him were happy.

Jessi was still shaken but tried to compose herself. "Hey Gary," she said, offering a weak smile, "Yeah, what's up?"

Gary suddenly looked concerned. "Are you okay? What's wrong? I don't believe in the time I've known you that I've ever seen you look like you'd seen a ghost."

"Um, yeah," she replied, knowing she couldn't hide this from her boss. "I just got a really disturbing phone call."

"Oh?" Gary said and sat down in the chair across from her. "Who was it from? Not a dissatisfied client, I hope?"

"I don't know who it was from," Jessi said. "They were using some kind of voice changer. It was really creepy. "I've heard about calls like this but never received one. I really have no idea what it was all about."

"Were you threatened?" Gary asked. "Should we call the police? I don't like having my employees stalked or crank calls coming into our place of business."

"I'm not sure if we should contact the police. It was only one call. Maybe if they call again. I don't think I was being threatened. This guy was just being creepy, is all. I don't know. It's just bizarre."

Gary thought momentarily and then said, "I'll have my secretary look into it and see if we can figure out where it came from. We'll make out an incident report just to document it. Let me know if you receive any other calls like this, and we'll get the police on it right away. I don't want my employees harassed."

"Thank you, Gary," Jessi said. "I appreciate it. So, did you need to see me about something, or did you just have a feeling that you should check up on me?"

Gary hit his forehead with the palm of his hand. "Oh, yeah! With all this disturbing news, I almost forgot why I came to see you! I have an assignment for you."

Jessi always liked it when Gary personally gave her an assignment. It made her feel like he really appreciated her work. And he did appreciate her and her work ethic. She reminded him of his granddaughter. He wanted to ensure she was taken care of and loved how she worked hard and enjoyed what she did for the company.

"Cool." She replied. "What is it?"

Gary handed her the paperwork, and she looked it over as he talked. "I've got a warehouse that needs appraising. I will send you out just to do the building and someone else to do the land appraisal. Our client owns both and wants to sell the whole kit and kaboodle. It's a large warehouse outside of town. He asked that we not put his name on the paperwork as he has a client interested in purchasing and wants to pay for the appraisal. Tax deduction, you know."

"Yeah, okay." Jessi was excited. "I can do that." These were some of the most straightforward yet challenging jobs. She had to pay attention to the details.

"I'd like you to run out and look at the building first," Gary continued, "then come back and do some research on its background. It's empty now, and the owner will leave it open for us. Seems he's too busy to come out and answer questions while we're there, but after I get your initial report, I'll call him with any questions. So, since it's empty, there shouldn't be much to look at. He said the main office is inside and stands alone in the middle of the warehouse. It will need to be looked at, but the rest is an open area. The owner wants to sell the building soon, so we'll need to work up an appraisal price for him within the next few days."

Jessi had been taking notes. She wanted to ensure she didn't miss anything when she went out. "Are the utilities on?" she asked.

"I think so. At least, I hope so. There is some plumbing inside, and since it's been vacant for about a year, I would hate to see frozen pipes. Although the owner might have had the water cut off. I'll call and ask before you go out."

"Okay. Thank you. Anything else?"

"Oh, yeah," he said as an afterthought, "I want you to take Erin with you and teach her more about what you do and how you do it. You're one of our best, and I think she could learn a lot from you."

Jessi beamed at the compliment and blushed slightly knowing she was not only allowed to train but she would also get to spend more time with her best friend.

"Thanks, Gary," she said. "I appreciate you trusting me like that. It will be a nice way to wrap up the week. Since we need to finish this fairly quickly, do you want me to work on it this weekend?"

"Are you kidding?" Gary said smiling, "The weekends are meant to be enjoyed, and coming to work, no matter how much you like it, is not the way to enjoy it. I want you to go out and have a great time this weekend and not worry about work. Get all the necessary stuff done today and then come in early on Monday to wrap it up. I'm sure our client can wait until then for his numbers."

Gary stood up and walked to the door. He turned before he left and said, "I'll let you know what, if anything, we find out about that phone call. Just be careful and let me know if you get any other calls like that."

"I will. Thank you, Gary!" Jessi had thought about telling Gary about the previous night in the parking lot but then decided that the incident would never happen again, so she just let it drop. But she also wondered about John. He didn't seem to be anywhere in the building today, but they weren't friends, so she hadn't thought to ask if John was in today. She shrugged. *Nothing to worry about.* She was sure he had learned his lesson and would never bother her again.

Jessi started gathering what she would need to evaluate the building. She grabbed her paperwork, measuring wheel, and other supplies. After about half an hour, she was almost ready to go with everything packed, stacked, and preliminary research completed. Just as she stood to begin taking things to her car, Erin burst into the office very excited.

"Hey!" she said to Jessi. "I get to go with you today! Teach me, oh wise one. I am putty in your hands. Shape me into the next great appraiser." Erin raised her hands into the air and bowed down in mock worship.

Jessi laughed. "I heard they were sending someone with me. Is it you? Really? Huh, that's a surprise. Why would they send you and not John? Oh, wait, because John's an idiot. That's right. I forgot. Maybe I should ask Jim to go with me. He is, after all, interested in going out with me."

Erin looked hurt and stuck out her bottom lip.

"I'm just teasing you," Jessi said. "Gary came in a little while ago and told me. "It's great, isn't it?"

"It will be fun. I can't wait to see what *this* warehouse looks like."

"We'll probably be there for a while," Jessi said. "It looks like it's fairly big. I just need to finish putting a few things together."

"Sounds good," Erin said. "Anything I can help you with?"

Jessi formed a devilish smile, then looked up at Erin, who took a step back.

"What?" she asked.

"Of course, you can help, my dear," Jessi said, standing and walking over to the pile of equipment, books, and papers that she had been creating. "You can carry this, and this, and this…"

She started piling things into Erin's waiting arms. Books, papers, clipboards, pens, and anything else she could find. Once Erin's arms were full and the pile was up to her chin, Jessi looked around the room. She put her hands on her hips and said, "Well, I think that should do it. Let's go." Jessi marched out the door empty-handed.

"Wait," Erin shouted, struggling to walk and see simultaneously. "What are you bringing?"

Jessi stopped and looked back at her friend. "I'm bringing you, silly. That's *my* job. You asked if you could help with anything."

"I didn't ask to help with everything, though," she grumbled.

"If you were doing this alone, you would carry all of this to your car. Remember, you are putty in my hands, and I am shaping you into the best. It takes much work to become the best, grasshopper. I will make you the best. Just keep remembering that and say it over and over to yourself, 'I will be the best. I will be the best.'" Jessi continued the mantra as she walked down the hallway. Erin grumbled and staggered down the hall, following her teacher, grumbling, "I will be the best. I will be the best. I will be the stupid best…"

# CHAPTER 8

## MURDER

The drive to the warehouse took about twenty minutes. Jessi and Erin talked about everything. They always had things to discuss. They were like sisters. They had known each other all their lives and could almost complete each other's sentences. "We need to be careful when we talk about what I can hear and not hear," Jessi said.

"What do you mean?" Erin asked.

"Yesterday, when John was doing his stupid macho stuff, he talked about me hearing future sounds. I've never told anyone at work about that. You and I are the only ones that I know of who know about it."

"And John," Erin said.

"But that's what I can't figure out. How did he know?"

"I wondered about that too," Erin said thoughtfully. "I have no idea. We never discuss it at work, so I'm unsure how he would know. A few people at school knew. Maybe Jim said something."

Jessi thought. "No, I don't think it would have been Jim. They didn't seem to know or like him."

"True," Erin said thoughtfully.

"Maybe it was someone from outside of work that they know.

"But it would have to be someone who knows you well," Erin said.

"It's a real mystery. I never wanted to let anyone else know. And now it seems more and more people know. I imagine no one will care if I don't have to use it. And even if everyone knew, I could always deny it and turn it around. I could just call *them* crazy!"

Erin laughed. "That's the best plan you've had yet," Erin said, looking out the window. "Is that the warehouse?" She pointed at a large building in the middle of a spacious, isolated field.

"I think so. It looks like it," Jessi said. "Here we go!"

They pulled into the warehouse parking lot.

"So, about the phone call you got at the office," Erin said.

Jessi put the car in park. "I don't want to talk about it anymore."

"Talking about it might help you figure it out. It might help you remember the little details you aren't remembering."

Jessi opened the door and got out of the car. "There's nothing else to say about it."

But when they got out of the car, the conversation continued.

"I'm just saying it's weird," Erin said. "Why would anyone call you and say the things he said? More importantly, who was it? Were you able to recognize anything about the voice? Anything about the way they talked?"

"Not a thing," Jessi said, "It was only a few sentences before I hung up the phone. I probably should have kept him on the phone longer to see if I could figure it out, but it freaked me out. And I had to wonder about the whole enclosed spaces remark. I'm not claustrophobic and never have been, but just how he said it gave me the chills."

"And you're sure you don't know who it was?"

"I'm sure I would tell you if I even suspected, but I don't. He used one of those voice changer things." Jessi put her hand over her mouth and began breathing in and out heavily, mimicking Darth Vader, "Watch out for enclosed spaces, Luke..."

They both laughed. Then Erin had a thought. "If they used a voice changer, you wouldn't even know if it was a man or a woman, would you?"

"Hadn't thought about it, but no. That makes it even creepier. But let's stop talking about that and get to work."

Jessi walked to the back of her car and opened the trunk. She took out the measuring wheel, some forms, pens, and a clipboard. She handed the clipboard to Erin, and they walked over to the building. As they were walking, Jessi stopped suddenly.

"What is it?" Erin asked.

"I just had a thought," Jessi said. "If I couldn't tell whether it was a man or a woman, maybe you did it." Jessi smiled and continued walking.

"What!" Erin exclaimed. "You don't honestly think I would ever do anything like that to you, do you?"

"Of course not, silly."

"Good, 'cause I think you know me well enough to know I might pull a joke on you now and then, but never something like that."

"I don't know," Jessi said. "You've pulled some pretty good ones on April Fool's Day and during Halloween."

"But it's neither of those days, and I wouldn't do something like this," Erin said.

"I know. I'm just messing with you. But I still have to wonder why someone would call me like that. I wondered if it might have been John. He *did* say that he'd get back at me. But I don't think he's bright enough to pull something like this."

The two women walked over to the corner of the building. Jessi opened and extended her measuring wheel, set the wheel to zero, and set it on the ground.

"Why do you use this antique piece of equipment?" Erin asked.

"It makes me feel good. It's comfortable. I could use a laser measuring instrument, but I like getting extra steps in. Good for the heart!"

"I guess," Erin said, sounding bored. "So what are you going to do?"

"We need to get the square footage of the building," Jessi started. "Since it's a rectangular structure, we'll measure two sides and go from there."

"Ah," Erin said, looking thoughtfully at the sky. "Takes me back to Mrs. Harder's geometry class. I never thought I would be using anything from that class. It was always so boring."

"And here's your chance to brush off those cobwebs and reactivate some brain cells. I'll take the measurements and let you do the math. But Don't worry, I'll double-check your work."

"Oh, whatever!" Erin said. She clipped the papers onto the clipboard and walked next to Jessi as she measured.

"Why do you use these papers and pencils when you could be using a tablet?" Jessi chided.

"Takes me back to those days in High School," Erin said. "Besides, I forgot to bring my tablet. I thought you had packed everything, and low and behold, you didn't."

Jessi sighed. "Must I do everything for you?"

Both laughed! They were so focused on their work and conversation that they didn't notice the figure sneaking up behind them. He was quiet and worked hard to only stay on the grassy areas so that the gravel wouldn't give him away. He walked quietly but quickly and, when he was close enough, reached out with two hands, grabbing them on the shoulders.

Both girls jumped and screamed. Erin dropped her clipboard. Jessi raised her measuring wheel. They both turned around, ready to fight whoever was behind them. They were surprised to see Jim with a cowering and fearful look on his face, his hands up, ready to cover his face and head should the girls react violently to his prank.

"Uh, boo?" he said timidly.

The girls looked at him angrily. "What do you think you're doing?" Jessi yelled at him and smacked him on the chest.

Jim stuttered and stammered but could not get the words out. He felt terrible now. During the short time he spent planning the surprise, it seemed like a funny thing to do. He honestly didn't think beyond the sneaking up on them part. He thought all would be good, everyone would have a good laugh, and it would be business as usual.

Jessi continued when Jim didn't answer. "You don't just sneak up behind someone like that. You have the courtesy to say something and let them know you're there. Especially when you're sneaking up behind two women with martial arts training. What were you thinking? You're lucky we didn't kick the…"

Erin stopped her from continuing. "I think he gets the idea, Jess." Erin was actually feeling sorry for Jim at this point. She wasn't sure if he would pass out or get sick. All the color had drained from his face, and Erin could swear he was shaking ever so slightly.

"I am so sorry," Jim said. "I honestly didn't mean to startle you like that, Jessi. I just wanted to surprise you. Maybe you knew I was coming and would be watching for me. I'm so sorry."

"Oh, you surprised us all right!" Jessi huffed. She reset her measuring wheel to zero and pushed past Jim, heading back to the end of the building to start over. Jim watched her walk away, feeling terrible.

"Don't worry, Jim," Erin said. "She's just a little freaked out about something that happened at work today. She'll be okay."

"I…" Jim stammered, "I didn't know. I really feel like a jerk."

"I know. Just go over to her and try to start a normal conversation. No surprises this time. If you want to be her friend, be her friend. If you're looking for more, you must take your time. Start out with the friendship first. Get to know her, and who she is, then the jokes and surprises can come later. Okay?" Erin was sincerely feeling bad for Jim. He seemed so sweet, and she hoped Jessi would give him another chance. "Come on. I'll walk over with you, and let's try this again."

Jim and Erin walked over to Jessi. Jim was the first to speak.

"I'm sorry, Jessi. I only came to do the land evaluation for Gary. I saw you both over here and wanted to say hi to let you know I was here. I didn't mean to scare you."

Jessi whirled around to face Jim. "Scare me? *Scare me!* Do you seriously think that you could scare me? Startle maybe. Surprise, yes. But scare me? No, no, no. I do not scare. Not by anyone who sneaks up on me."

"How many times will I have to apologize to you today?" Jim asked. "I'm sorry. I didn't mean to use the word, scare. No, I don't think I could ever scare you." Jim felt a little put out and wondered if getting to know Jessi was worth all this trouble.

Jessi's expression softened, and she said, "Don't worry about it. And I'm sorry. I'm just a little jumpy today. But for the record, you startled me, and please, don't ever do it again. For your sake and mine. Perhaps someday you'll see what I can do if I need to."

Jim took a step back.

Jessi held up her hands. "No, not to you. Now *I'm* sorry. I'm not threatening you. I was just saying that someday I'll show you some moves I learned when getting my black belt."

"Wait. You're a black belt? That's impressive. I just thought that you knew a little martial arts. So you studied for what, a year or so?"

Jessi looked at Erin, who was shaking her head in disbelief. Jessi turned back to Jim and gently said, "I studied for seven years to get my black belt, Jim. I'm higher than that because I studied longer than the seven years required to get my black belt."

"I'm very impressed," Jim said. "That takes a lot of work and dedication. I'd love to learn more about it sometime."

Jessi felt better about Jim. He said some things that touched her heart. Maybe he wasn't such a bad guy after all. Time would tell.

"I appreciate that, Jim. Perhaps I overreacted a bit. It's been a strange morning."

"Yeah," Jim said. "Erin told me that you were a little upset, to begin with, and if I had known that, I would have been more sensitive about it. I hope you're feeling better now, though."

Jessi stopped what she was doing and gave Erin a dirty look. Erin shrugged. Jessi started measuring again while Erin and Jim followed behind.

"So, what's going on at the office that upset you?" Jim continued. "I'd like to help if I can."

"That's very sweet of you, Jim," Jessi said. "I really appreciate the offer, but I'm sure I can handle it. In fact, I really don't think it was that big of a deal now that I think about it. I just made it out to be more than…" Jessi stopped walking and talking when she heard a woman screaming. She lifted her head and listened, trying to find the direction from where the screams were coming.

Erin looked at Jessi. "What's up? Why are you stopping?"

Jessi listened to what the woman was screaming. There was a scuffle and the sound of things being knocked over. There were other voices that she couldn't make out. She heard yelling, and the woman screamed even louder,

"Help me! He's trying to kill me!"

Jessi dropped her measuring wheel and ran over to the warehouse entrance door. Jim and Erin looked at each other in surprise, then ran after her. When Jessi arrived at the door, she turned the knob and burst inside. She looked around and headed to the small structure in the middle of the empty building. She opened the door and looked inside. Nothing. The inside of the building was dark, except for the dim light coming in through the windows at the top of the walls. She was breathing hard, and her breathing was the only sound she could hear. She darted out of the office and looked around the dimly lit warehouse. She could barely see anything. As her eyes adjusted to the low light, she saw the tall, empty walls and the expansive concrete floor. It was empty. Her heart was pounding in her ears. She heard footsteps and turned to see Erin and Jim standing in the doorway. She continued to look around and listen but only heard the slight sounds of garbled talking that slowly faded away until there was only the sound of her breathing.

Jessi turned and looked at Erin. "Are you okay, Jess?"

Jessi turned back and stared into the semi-darkness of the warehouse. She knew what was going to happen. Erin walked up behind her and placed her hand on Jessi's shoulder. Jessi jumped, whirled around, and grabbed Erin by her shoulders.

"She's going to be murdered," Jessi whispered.

# CHAPTER 9

## WHAT NOW?

"What?" Erin asked. "Who? What are you talking about?"

"I don't know," Jessi said, "but I heard it. I heard her scream. I heard her begging for help and saying someone was trying to kill her. I heard other voices, too, saying things I couldn't make out. There was fighting, and then it faded away."

Erin's eyes widened. "Are you sure?"

"How often have you known me to be wrong about these things?" Jessi asked. "I heard it. She was being murdered. She was screaming. Someone is going to die here in twenty-four hours."

Jessi walked blindly outside. She felt numb. She didn't know what to do. Most of what she heard when she heard the future was very impersonal. Maybe a couple fighting occasionally, and the sirens, the accidents, and such didn't involve an individual person. This was a woman. A woman living out her life today and tomorrow would be dead. When the sunlight hit Jessi's face, she had to squint momentarily. When she turned to shield her eyes from the sun, she thought she saw someone disappear around the far corner of the building. "Did you see that?" Jessi asked Erin. "Over there," she pointed. "I thought I saw someone."

Jessi started to step in that direction but stopped when Jim ran out of the building. She continued staring at that corner, hoping to see whatever she saw before, but there was nothing. Whatever or whoever it was had vanished now, at least from her sight. *What a crazy few days it's been,* she thought to herself.

Jim could hardly contain himself. "Wow! So everything they say about you at work is true!" he exclaimed.

Jessi had reached that point where being patient was not an option. Not only had she never wanted anyone else to know about what she could do, other than Erin, but now Jim was implying that others at work take about it. She whirled around and looked at Jim. "And what, exactly, is it that they say about me at work?"

Jim's face flushed and he looked down, indicating he knew he had done it again. "Jessi, I would love to have the ability to keep my mouth shut, but God blessed me with a very loose jaw and a very active brain. I found out over the years that the two don't make a good combination," he stuttered. "Well, uh, you know. They say that you can hear things that happen in the future and stuff like that."

Jessi felt that Jim was about to be the source of heartache and pain. She pictured him returning to the office and confirming all of the rumors that had been started and suddenly becoming the authority on the freak. She had feared for most of the past few years she would be labeled crazy if word of her ability ever got out.

"Okay, here's the deal," Jessi said and took a deep breath. "I can hear things that happen in the future. Not all things, just traumatic life events. But you have to know if you plan on returning to the office and standing at the water cooler and telling everyone that…"

"It's so cool!" Jim interrupted. He turned to Erin. "Did you know about this? I mean, for real? Or did you just suspect like the rest of us? You guys are best friends, so you must have known. It's incredible! How have you been able to keep this a secret from everyone?"

Jessi was speechless. As she was growing up with this, she never dreamed that she'd receive this type of reaction.

Jim continued. "What a trip! What possibilities! Can you imagine what you could do with this ability? Just think, if you went to a horse race and could hear who would win the next heat, maybe you would not hear that, but you could hear the people traumatized by the loss or those who were excited because they won! Or, no, wait, even better, the stock market! You could hear which stocks would be huge before they were!"

Jim looked at Jessi, focusing on her. "How does it work?"

"What?" Jessi said, taken by surprise. "Excuse me?"

"How does it work? Can you hear things from far away, or is it like someone or something is right next to you? Is there distortion associated with the sounds? Do you see anything different when you hear things?"

Jessi held up her hands to stop the barrage of questions. "What are you talking about?" she asked. "Why are you asking me these things? Aren't you freaked out by this? Do you even believe it?"

Jim looked at Jessi. He was breathing hard and smiling. "Believe it? I just saw it happen. You're amazing! You've been blessed with an incredible talent. There's so much that you could do with this. I have a million questions. I can't even imagine what it would be like. It must be so cool to be able to do that!"

He hit the nerve, and Jessi became angry. "Cool? You think it's cool? How cool is it for people to think you're a freak or crazy? How cool is it for people to stare at you because they think you hear things that aren't there? Oh yeah, it's really cool to suddenly pull your car over in the middle of traffic because you hear a siren that *isn't there*!"

"I only meant that…"

"I don't care what you meant," Jessi shouted. "You don't know what it's like. And no, I couldn't go to a race track, or the stock market or a baseball field to hear tomorrow's scores because it only seems to happen before something tragic occurs, and believe me when I say that there is a lot of tragedy in this world, much of it that we never see. Cool? No. Not really. A blessing? More like a curse. Living with this has been the biggest curse ever. I wish that I had never been 'blessed' with this."

Jessi turned away when Jim said, "I'm sorry, Jessi. I was just interested in what happened to you before and what happened to you today. I was thinking that maybe in some way I could help."

Jessi stopped. The last time someone said they wanted to help her was when her mother took her to the audiologist. That turned out terrible. But that was six years ago, and this wasn't her mother. She wasn't sure what to do or say, but she was convinced that standing behind her was a friend who cared and wanted to help. Her face softened, and she turned back around to face Jim.

"How could you help?" she asked. "What could you possibly do to help me?"

"I could help you find a way to stop the murder," he said.

It had been a glancing thought, but she didn't think about what it would entail to try and prevent this from happening. Now she started to think. How would she do this? An argument was one thing, but this was murder. Someone was going to lose their life. She should try to stop it, but how? Who would believe her?

"How could you do that?" she asked.

"I know a few people in the media. Television, actually. My sister-in-law, my brother's wife, works for Channel 7 downtown. I'm sure she would help us."

An awkward silence filled the air between them, and Jessi felt terrible that she hadn't given Jim a chance. Conversely, Jim felt bad that he wasn't more sensitive to Jessi's needs.

"Would she even believe us?" Jessi asked. "Most people don't believe that I can do this."

"Let's just say she's heard some amazing things in her job. I think that she'll listen to us, at the very least. Beyond that, I can't say, but she knows me and knows I wouldn't talk to her about something that doesn't ring true."

Jessi needed clarification. She didn't want the world to know what she could do. She was afraid of what people would say and do. She went silent.

Jim broke the silence. "So, have you been able to hear the future all of your life?"

"No," Jessi replied. "There was an incident on a bus several years ago when I was going to a Kung Fu demonstration. Erin was there."

"Yeah," Erin said. "I remember it like it was yesterday. The bus got hit and rolled, and Jessi was really hurt."

"Hurt?" Jim said, concerned. "How badly were you hurt?"

Both girls answered at the same time but with different answers. Erin said, "She died." While Jessi answered, "Not bad."

Jessi felt she should have a glaring look pasted on her face whenever she looked at Erin today. It seemed she had glared at her a lot and felt another one coming on.

"I really don't remember a lot about the accident itself. I wasn't conscious between the accident and when I arrived at the hospital. The only thing I remember about it is that it changed my life." Jessi said.

"Well," Erin chimed in, "we were sitting together. It was just you and I in that row of seats. I saw you. You were dead. They revived you in the ambulance. They wouldn't let us go with you because we all had to be checked out, but you were dead. You weren't breathing, and you didn't respond to anything."

The two girls locked eyes briefly until Jim said, "Well, you look pretty good now."

The tension shattered like a large pane of glass. Everyone burst out laughing. It took a bit before the laughter died away, but when it did, Jim asked, "So, getting back to what you hear. Does everything you hear come true? I mean, do you really think this murder will happen?"

Jessi looked sad. "That's the bad part. Yeah. I hate it. It's awful knowing that something will happen but not being able to see it, ya know? You'd be amazed at how deceiving sounds can be. You hear a squeak, and it could be anything. A car door opening, squeaky brakes... and I don't know what it is until the next day. Sometimes, I never find out. I just have to guess what it might have been."

Jim thought, "I never thought about it that way. It would almost be like you were blind, but only sometimes." He sighed and then looked up at Jessi.

"So, where do we start?"

"Start?" Jessi asked. "Start what?"

"We need to stop this murder, and I want to be a part of it. I feel you'll need as many people on your side with this as possible." Jim said.

"He's got a point," Erin said, "It would be good to have a few more people to help with this. After all, how do you convince people that a murder will happen unless you're the one planning it?"

"Good point," Jim said.

"Seems like everyone has good points in this conversation," Jessi sighed.

"So we need input from other people, but who do you think will help us?"

They thought momentarily, and Erin said, "I'm supposed to meet Barry tonight for dinner. Why don't the two of you meet us at Yasutaka's Sushi House, and we can plot and plan."

Jessi pulled out her cell phone and looked at the time. "We must ensure we have something done by three-fifty tomorrow afternoon. It's always twenty-four hours exactly after I hear the sounds that the event happens, so we need to be sure we have someone here before then."

Jim's eyes lit up. "So, we'll meet you at the sushi house tonight. Like a date?"

"Not a date," Jessi said.

"But *like* a date?" Jim insisted.

"A meeting," Jessi said.

"Oh, for goodness sake," Erin said. "We're wasting time. Just call it a date and be done with it!"

"But it's…" Jessi was flustered.

"A date then!" Jim said quickly.

Erin grabbed Jessi by the arm and dragged her over to the car.

"See you tonight then, Jim!" Erin called out. "Thank you for helping!"

Jim stood looking bewildered and then called out, "Hey! What time should we meet?"

"I'll take my car, Jim, and see you there," Jessi yelled.

"Six-thirty," Erin hollered. "See you tonight!"

The girls got into Jessi's car and started it. Jessi looked at Erin. "It's not a date!"

Erin smiled and shrugged. "At least we're finally going out on a double meeting."

Jessi put the car into gear and drove off.

Feeling light as a feather and giddy as a schoolboy, Jim jogged over to his car. He jumped in the air and let out a shout of victory! He climbed into his car and drove off to prepare for his date.

At the other end of the warehouse, a person clad in dirty tennis shoes, old jeans, and a ripped t-shirt rounded the corner. The mysterious person watched as the cars sped away. A newspaper dropped to the ground by the tennis shoes as the person turned and walked away. The headline on the paper's front page read, "Blue Mountain Slasher Still at Large."

# CHAPTER 10

## THE PLAN

Barry and Erin have been seeing each other for about a year. He is a good-looking young man. His sandy blonde hair made him look like a young boy, always ready to pull a prank. Tonight, he and Erin were dressed casually.

"I like your shirt," Erin said. "The blue really sets off your eyes. Is it new?"

"I know," Barry said. "Yeah. I bought it today just for tonight. I'm glad you like it. I bought it just because I thought it would make my eyes look good."

"Glad you're not disappointed," Erin said sarcastically. "Maybe we should see what we want to eat before Jessi gets here."

They sat at a table in the sushi house and looked at their menus. Erin looked down at the table and her phone. *Six-twenty-five.* She told Jim six-thirty to give her and Barry some time to talk before they arrived. Erin hadn't talked about Jessi and what Barry needed to know yet. She didn't know how to approach the subject in a way that Barry would understand.

Erin had never told Barry about Jessi's ability. She wasn't sure if Jessi knew this, but Erin had promised to keep it a secret, and she was not only true to her word but true to her friend as well. She looked up every time a person entered the restaurant and finally saw Jessi walk in. She held up her hand and waved. Jessi looked around for a moment before finally seeing Erin's flailing arm. She smiled and walked over to the table.

"Hey, Erin," Jessi said and pulled out a chair. "How are you, Barry?" she asked, sitting down.

"Hey there, beautiful," Barry said. "Erin tells me you have a guy meeting you here. Anyone I know?"

"I don't think so," Jessi said.

"How come I've never met this guy? Is he your boyfriend?"

"No, Barry. He's not my boyfriend," Jessi sighed.

"Leave her alone, Barry. You'll meet him soon enough, and you can have another new person to tell all about your ventures and adventures," Erin said.

"Just watch for him. He's kind of nerdy-looking. You can't miss him."

Jim was not as easily recognized as Erin described when he entered the restaurant. At work, he always dressed conservatively and, yes, a little nerdy. He would button up his shirts to the neck, wore glasses, and even a pocket protector. Tonight, he wasn't dressed that way at all. In fact, one might say he was almost good-looking, with a definite sense of style. Rather than being slicked back, his hair was tussled and freshly washed, and he wasn't wearing his glasses. So it was no wonder no one from Jessi's table waved when he came in.

It took him a moment, but he finally saw his party and walked over to the table. Jessi and Erin looked up.

"Jim?" Jessi asked.

"In the flesh," he replied. "Mind if I sit down?"

"No, no," Jessi said, blushing slightly, "not at all. Please, sit here." She indicated the chair next to her.

Jim sat down next to Jessi, and Erin nudged her a little with her elbow when she pretended to drop her napkin.

Jim looked at Barry. "I'm Jim, by the way."

"I'm so sorry," Erin said, "I forgot that you haven't met. Jim, this is my boyfriend, Barry. Barry, Jim."

The two shook hands.

Barry got right to the point, turning to Jessi. "Erin's been telling me that you need help with something of great importance. So, Jess. What is it?"

"Yeah," Jessi said nervously, glancing at Erin. "Has she told you anything about what's going on?"

"Not really," Barry said. "She wanted to wait and let you explain things. She said it would be better if you gave me the details, thus the reason I asked you what's going on. So, what's going on?"

"Actually," Jessi said, "I need to run to the bathroom for a sec. Come with me, Erin."

Jessi stood, and Erin went along. She was sure Jessi wanted to be updated on how much Barry knew. "Be right back," Erin said.

"Don't be gone too long!" Jim said.

Jim looked at his hand, thinking about the recent handshake with Barry. Barry's hand seemed soft, so Jim was sure that Barry wasn't in construction or anything similar. His first impression of Barry was that he was a leader, but seeing how quiet he was now, he wasn't sure. Jim decided to take the lead.

"How long have you known Erin, Barry?

"We've been seeing each other for about a year now. How about you and Jess?"

"Well, we've worked together for a while at Thompson Appraisals, and I knew her back in middle school, but this is the first time we've gone out. I've always wanted to go out with her, so tonight is a special event."

"Yeah. Erin and I met at a movie theater. We were going to see the same movie. She had bought some popcorn and left it on her seat while she went to buy something else. I walked in and saw the abandoned popcorn and just figured that someone left it there for me. So I picked it up, sat down, and started eating it. Needless to say, when she got back, she was a little upset that I was eating her popcorn. I told her that I wasn't very happy either because the popcorn didn't have enough butter. I handed it back to her and said that she should go get some butter on it. She said that maybe I should go and get it, so I stood up, took the popcorn, and went back out to the lobby, got the butter, and came back. When I sat down next to her, she seemed like she was really mad, but then I offered her some buttered popcorn, and she was really happy. We talked for a while and watched the movie together. I got her number, and bam! Here we are today. Weird, huh?"

Jim couldn't believe what he was hearing. He just stared at Barry.

"Incredibly weird," he said.

"Yeah, she is," Barry said, "incredible, I mean."

In the meantime, Jessi and Erin entered the bathroom.

"How much does he know?" Jessi asked.

"You mean about what you can do?"

"Yes. Of course, that's what I mean. What have you told him?"

"I haven't told him anything, Jess. I told you I would never tell anyone, and I haven't. I felt it would be better to wait and let you tell him as much or as little as you thought best."

"I appreciate it, Erin," Jessi said. "I'm still uncomfortable telling him anything, but if he's going to help, he'll probably need to know at least a little." Jessi had to decide how much was enough or too much. "Let's head back out."

Jim looked around to see if the girls were on their way back and finally saw them coming. They sat back down at the table.

"Sorry to take so long," Jessi said.

"No worries," Jim said. I was just getting to know Barry a little and listening to his riveting stories."

Jessi looked a little skeptical and was speechless.

Jim turned back toward Barry and asked, "So what do you do for a living, Barry?"

Jessi and Erin groaned simultaneously.

Barry perked up at the question and said, "I own my own company. We have a line of video games that have really taken off. Several big-name companies have asked us to create games for them. Do you play video games, Jim?"

As Barry asked this question, Erin reached over and touched Barr y's hand.

"Let's talk about that later, Barry. We have some important things to discuss."

"Important?" Barry said. "More important than video games?"

"I don't mind talking about your work sometimes, but you always talk about these video games lately. You don't talk about anything else."

Barry suddenly became offended, and it could be heard in his voice.

"Those *video games* are our future. You should be more grateful that I'm a natural salesman. We are going to be rich someday because of them."

"Uh huh," Erin said, looking bored.

"Hey guys," Jessi said, trying to pull the conversation back on track.

"We've got a huge problem here to discuss, remember? Can we please talk about the video games another time?"

Jim broke in,"Yeah. Maybe we can talk about the games later tonight, Barry. I'm really interested in what you do. Give me your card, and maybe you and I can go out for a coffee sometime and talk about your company if we don't get the time tonight!"

Barry grumbled, "Thank you, Jim!" He handed Jim a business card. "At least you appreciate what I do. It's so hard to get Erin to understand how important…"

"Barry!" Erin said sternly.

An angry silence halted all conversations temporarily at the table. Barry and Erin locked eyes and then didn't look at each other at all. Jim and Jessi glanced helplessly at each other. No one knew what to do or say to get things moving again.

"So," Jim said, trying to continue the conversation. "I called my sister-in-law and told her we might have a hot lead for her. She was slightly interested in meeting with us but went through all the polite rhetoric, saying 'yeah' and and 'okay' and just kind of led me on. That is, of course, until I said the magic word, murder!"

"Wait, what?" Barry perked up. "Murder?" He looked at Erin. "You didn't say anything about murder." Barry's voice was rising to an uncomfortable level, and some people at surrounding tables were beginning to look. "I'm a pretty open guy, but if we're talking murder, I'm not sure I want to be a part of it. Why didn't you tell me this meeting was about murder, Erin?"

"Shhh," Erin said to Barry. "Keep your voice down." Erin gave Jim a dirty look.

"What?" Jim asked. "I believe in getting straight to the point." Jim looked around at the people who were staring and looking concerned. "It's okay," he announced to the crowd. "Sorry to disturb you. We're going over the lines to a new play we're writing, and Barry, here, tends to get into character too much sometimes. We'll keep it down. Sorry to bother you all. Enjoy your meals!"

People slowly went back to their conversations and to their own little worlds.

Jessi shook her head. "Okay, well, since the cat is out and we've gotten to the point, let's figure out what to do next. We've only got about twenty-one hours to stop this from happening."

If Barry was confused before, the last statement didn't help. He started quickly rapping on the table with his knuckles and waving with his other hand. Jessi and Jim found this sight very humorous and tried not to laugh.

"Twenty-one hours?" Barry asked. "Okay, let's back up the information train and let poor old Barry get on. Someone let it pull out of the station before Barry got his ticket. What is going on here?"

"Sorry, hun," Erin said. "Let me explain."

"I wish you would!" Barry said. "I really wish you would because if you want my help, then I kinda need to know what I'm helping with, you know?"

Erin glared at Barry and thought about continuing the conversation with Jim but decided she would be kind one moment longer. She looked at Jim.

"Maybe you should explain, Jim. Now *I* have to use the bathroom. Coming, Jess?"

The two girls once again got up from the table. Jessi looked at Jim and shrugged just as Erin grabbed her by the arm and hauled her away.

"Those women have the smallest bladders I've ever seen," Barry said, shaking his head. "So Jim, my new friend. What is this all about?"

"How much do you know about Jessi?" Jim asked.

"Whoa, whoa. If you're going to tell me she kills people, then just excuse me now and give my best to the ladies 'cause I'm out of here!"

Jim laughed. "No, Barry. That's not what I'm going to tell you. But sit back and listen well because you might have some trouble believing what you're about to hear."

Erin pushed Jessi through the bathroom door and followed her inside. She started pacing and walked over to the mirror. She turned to Jessi, opened her mouth, and closed it without saying a word. She put her hand up to her head and rubbed her forehead, trying to ward off a headache.

"What is wrong with you tonight?" Jessi asked.

"I don't know," Erin said. "I really don't know. Barry's being so weird, and I have no idea why."

"Uh huh," Jessi said. "What is he doing that you think is weird? Seems perfectly normal to me, or at least as normal as Barry can be."

"I can't put my finger on it, but he's just not himself all of a sudden. Everything was fine before you and Jim got here, then he just changed. He got…"

"Weird?" Jessi asked.

"Yeah. Exactly!" Erin said distractedly.

"Well," Jessi said, turning on the water in the sink, "you know my thoughts on Barry."

"Yes, and I don't care to hear them again."

"And yet," Jessi said, washing her hands, "I believe you shall hear them anyway since you have taken me captive in the woman's lavatory." She did her best British accent.

"No, please, Jessi," Erin begged, but Jessi continued without mercy.

"I think he's always been weird, and I've never really had a good feeling about him," Jessi said. "I feel that he doesn't treat you well, that he's an inconsiderate lout, and that he's been that way since the first day you met. Either he's a lout or just obtuse, or both."

"At least you're being kinder than you were the last time we talked about him," Erin moped.

"Yes, and I'm not sure why that is," Jessi said.

"Perhaps," Erin retorted, "it's because you have had so many good, solid relationships in your life. Let's see, how many have there been? Oh, that's right, none."

"Yeah, yeah. Touché. So why did you drag me in here?" Jessi thought they needed to get things moving.

"Jess," Erin looked very serious and then looked away. "Barry's been up to something, and I don't know what it is."

"Like something at work or something else?"

"I'm not sure," Erin said, turning back around. "I really don't know. Maybe it's just my imagination. Maybe I'm just being possessive. Maybe I'm just being selfish. He's just not paying as much attention to me as he used to. He's always so, well, so preoccupied."

"I never thought I would defend him," Jessi said, "but he is awfully set on keeping his business going. It sounds like he's pretty preoccupied with that."

"That's just it, Jess," Erin said, "His business is doing terrible. He puts on a great show for everyone else, but in reality, he doesn't know what he will do to pull it all together."

"Maybe that's it," Jessi said. "Guys are like that, you know. Maybe he's just worried about things with the business and tells you the superficial parts of it. Eventually, he'll tell you the whole story, but for now, he probably just doesn't want you to worry. In the meantime, you can always talk to or give him space or dump him and start over."

Erin looked up at Jessi in shock. "What did you say?"

"Kidding," Jessi said. "I wanted to see if you were even listening. Let's get back before the guys start going out together and forget about us!"

The girls left the bathroom and walked back to the table. They could see that the men were discussing something in low voices, and when the girls approached the table, the talking stopped completely. The boys didn't look up at the girls, nor did they look at each other. Instead, they suddenly found great interest in the plain white tablecloth directly under their elbows. Jessi and Erin sat down, and the waiter approached the table.

"Are you ready to order, or do you need a little more time?" the waiter asked.

"I think we're going to need some more time," Barry said abruptly.

"I'll come back," the waiter sniffed and walked off.

Once again, the table fell silent. Jessi and Erin looked at each other, wondering what was happening.

"So," Jessi said, "what's going on?"

Barry looked at Erin. "Why haven't I known about this?"

"About what?" Erin asked cautiously.

"About the thing that Jessi does, this, this hearing thing."

Jessi sighed. "I don't like it to be common knowledge. I've always asked Erin to keep it a secret, and she's always done that for me. Somehow, recently, it seems to be leaking out more and more. I'm not sure from where, but it is." She looked up at Erin, who was giving her a look of surprise.

"I know it's not you, Erin," Jessi said, "it's just that people find out and tell others until it grows into some ugly rumor that's only half-filled with truth. It leaks and then oozes and then runs all over everything, and people want to get it out of their lives because it's something that they can't deal with, don't believe, or want to make fun of."

Barry huffed. "Funny how it never seemed to leak toward me."

"I'm sorry, baby. I couldn't betray Jessi's trust in me," Erin said.

"So you felt like you couldn't trust me? Is that it?" Barry said.

Jessi stepped in. "Hey, look, it's not her fault, so don't take it out on her. Erin and I have been friends a heck of a lot longer than you two have known each other. And people don't exactly jump up and down when they find out about this. Well, except for Jim. But think about it, Barry. Look how you're acting right now. Not very nice and certainly not the first person I would ever share this with."

Barry stared at Jessi for a moment. Everyone at the table could tell he was trying to process what Jessi was saying and the situation. Finally, his face softened, and he looked back and forth from Jessi to Erin.

"You're right," he said to Jessi. Then he turned to Erin. "I'm sorry, honey. Guess I just let my ego get a little hurt. You're a good friend to Jessi; I'm glad I know about it now." He turned to Jessi and said, "You're also a good friend, and I appreciate you. I'm glad I know about it now, and I'll try to listen and learn how I can help."

"Okay, sweetie," Erin said in her little girl's voice.

"You know I love it when you talk that way to me. It drives me crazy."

"Gross!" Jessi exclaimed. "Let's save the gushy stuff for later. Time is ticking away here, and we're no closer to getting a plan than we were when we all first got here."

Jim, who had been sitting quietly observing, leaned forward with a solemn look on his face. "Guys, look." he started, "First of all, we're getting way off track here. We have something important to solve, and we can only solve it together. We need to focus on what's going on and determine what part each of us will play in preventing the loss of life. Second, we must be more covert about how we go about this. We aren't the only ones who know about what's going to happen, so I would suggest that we all remember where we are, how many people are around, and what we came to do. Let's speak softly before we blow it. For all we know, the killer could be here tonight. If that's the case, we could be next."

Jim brought up a thought that hadn't occurred to anyone at the table. They had no idea who the killer might be. For all they knew, the killer could be getting the idea of killing someone at the warehouse from their conversation. Jessi never really thought about what events led up to the fulfillment of the sound prophecies she heard, but now she wondered if she might inadvertently have something to do with setting this murder up. She shook the thought from her mind.

"You're right, Jim. I agree. We need to speak quietly and get a good solid plan quickly," Jessi said.

"I agree as well," Erin said. "What do you say, Barry. Truce for now? We can pick up apologizing later. It'll be fun!"

"I suppose," Barry pouted, "but I get to apologize first."

"No, I do, you big beautiful man."

"Ugh!" Jessi objected. "We're going backward. Let's discuss what needs to be done."

Jim cleared his throat. "Okay, good. So here's what we have so far. Jessi heard a woman's screams about three-thirty this afternoon, so we know that the killer will be getting things ready sometime before then, luring his victim to that spot."

"What if the killer already has her and plans to take her to the warehouse tomorrow?" Barry added.

"I didn't think about that," Jessi said. "What if it's all been set in motion? He could be anywhere and have anyone. This is just creepy thinking about it."

"Obviously, we can't stop the killer from kidnapping his victim, whether he's already done it or not," Erin said, "so we need to focus our efforts on stopping the murder at the warehouse and not worry about anything else. I don't know about you guys, but since we don't know who, what, or how many we're dealing with, I wouldn't feel comfortable just going to the warehouse and sitting and waiting."

"Yeah," Jessi said. "We don't even know how he's planning on killing her. If he has a gun, we could all end up dead. I heard other voices but couldn't make out what was being said."

Barry stated the obvious. "As I see it, the logical thing to do would be to go to the police and let them handle it. They have the manpower and the firepower to care for things like this."

Jim made a rude sound, getting the attention of the others. "Not that I mean to be rude, Barry, but let's think this through for a moment. We go to the police and say there will be a murder at the warehouse. The next thing they'll want to know is how we know this? We tell them that our friend, Jessi, heard the murder. Then we wait patiently while they contact the men in white coats to come and get us, take us away, and lock us up until further notice."

"Maybe we could tell them we got a tip," Barry suggested.

"Then they'll want to know where this tip came from. How are we involved in this? Why are we getting tips before the police? Do you see the suspicion this would raise? I would love nothing more than having the police there, but I don't want to be considered a suspect."

"Jim brings up some good points," Erin said. "I don't think I'd want to be in that position either."

"But I still think it's worth a try," Barry huffed. "If we're not guilty, then we shouldn't be implicated. Besides, the police are looking for that Blue Mountain Killer dude, and they might be willing to follow any leads they have, no matter how absurd they are. There are psychics always calling in leads."

"And the police don't always follow up on them right away," Jim said. "They have a limited number of officers available and can't be everywhere at once. No, we would have to make them understand that this is life if they get there by a certain time and death if they don't."

"I don't know," Erin said thoughtfully. "Now I think that Barry has a good point too. They *are* looking for a killer on the loose right now. They might be willing to listen to us."

"Everyone can have a good point, Erin," Jessi said. "But only one point can be valid, and being willing to listen to us and doing something about it are two different things. Besides, what if they listen and get there too late. Who are their first suspects? Us! Then they want to know everything. We get in trouble when it's not what they want to hear."

"How about this," Barry broke in. "Tomorrow morning, Erin and I can go to the police station. We'll tell them what we know and see what they can do. And no, Jessi, we won't mention that you heard the sounds. We'll play it cool and tell them that we overheard a conversation or something like that, and we were worried and thought they should check it out. Then, Jessi and Jim can explore other avenues and pursue other ideas. What do you think?"

"That sounds like a good idea. Jim?" Jessi said.

"I guess so. I hope this works," Jim said. "You and I can see my sister-in-law and see if she can help."

"Your sister-in-law?" Erin asked.

"She works at channel 7. I think she can help us get some help at the very least," Jim said.

"Is she like a news reporter or something?" Barry asked.

"Something like that," Jim said. "She's done a little reporting in her time."

Jessi wondered what that meant and if she could help at all or if this was a way for Jim to spend more time with Jessi.

At the end of the conversation, the waiter walked over and stood patiently. When Erin looked up at him, he said, "Are we ready to order yet?"

Barry looked at everyone at the table. "Special, okay?" he asked. Everyone nodded. "I guess we'll have four specials." He told the waiter, who nodded and walked off.

Jessi asked Jim, "So Jim, what do you think our plan should be for tomorrow?"

"Well, I think we should head to channel 7 and talk with my sister-in-law. I know that she won't have much time, but she might be able to do something to help."

"She works on Saturdays?" Jessi asked.

"Yeah," Jim said. "She is there a lot and has to be there most of the day. I'm sure that she'll appreciate the break."

"What do you think she can do to help?" Jessi asked, wondering if his sister-in-law was a receptionist or something.

"You'd be surprised what a television reporter can do when motivated by a story. An outstanding story!" Barry said.

"Well," Jim hesitated. "She's not exactly a reporter, but I'm sure she has some connections."

*I knew it,* Jessi thought to herself, *a receptionist.* Jessi gulped her water and attempted a smile, but it came out more of a sour sneer. She looked away and prayed that something would happen to save this poor girl. She wondered how seriously Jim took it. Was he only doing this to spend time with her? She hoped this wasn't the case. She liked him but would like him more if he was serious about what she had heard. He needed to take this seriously. He sounded sincere, but was he actually feeling that way? Tomorrow would tell. She decided to try to enjoy the evening and save the decision-making about this man for the morning.

None of them saw the man at the corner table listening intently to the entire conversation. He tossed his napkin on the floor, left money on the table, and walked quickly to the exit.

# CHAPTER 11

## INTRUDER

Jessi jumped at the sound of the blaring alarm. She hit the button on top of the clock and rolled to her back. "Wait a minute," she said aloud, pushing herself up on one arm. "Isn't it Saturday? Why did I set my…" The situation of the day hit her. She plopped back down on the bed and stared at the ceiling. "Oh yeah. The murder."

Saying the word out loud made it more real and ominous. It seemed fitting since, for some reason, it also seemed more personal. "Maybe because it was a woman who screamed," she said to the air.

Something was nagging her about this particular sound. She couldn't put her finger on it. It was like trying to recall a name that you've known all of your life except for this one moment. It's there, but it's not there. If it were solid, you could almost grab it. A dream woke her up throughout the night, and the nagging thought flitted in and out of her dreams. Each time she awoke, it would have folded itself back into her subconscious, escaping recognition.

She had hit snooze out of habit, and the radio quietly came on to tickle her eardrums. She didn't realize she had fallen back into deep sleep. But as the music played and the cheerful DJs cracked jokes; eventually, the life of day pulled away the cover of sleep. She opened her eyes and wiped away the blur of the night while trying to read the time. "Who gets up at 7:03 on a Saturday morning?" she said out loud to no one in particular. She turned off the radio and, forgetting about the night's worries, started falling back asleep. Then a loud noise from the other room started her heart beating hard and fast in her chest, throwing open her eyes and heightening every sense. She sat upright in bed and wondered if the sound was real or something imagined.

She slowly climbed out of bed and carefully walked to her bedroom door. She opened it slightly and peeked out down the hallway. She couldn't see anyone, so she slowly pulled the door open. She crept into the short hallway toward the living room and kitchen area. She strained to listen. She tried to hear any slight sound that might be the brushing of feet on the carpet or a small drop of sweat hitting the floor. She could see the front door as she reached the end of the hallway. It was slowly closing on its own. She crept out, looking in the kitchen and the living room. *Thank goodness it's a small apartment,* she thought to herself. When convinced that no one would spring out and grab her, she walked over and closed the front door. Just as she was about to lock it, there was a knock. She jumped, took a deep breath, and closed her eyes to focus. "Who is it?" she called out.

The voice from the other side of the door was much too cheery for this time on a Saturday morning. "It's Jim! Are you ready to go?"

Jessi sighed a big sigh of relief and opened the door.

Jim looked at Jessi. "I guess you're not quite ready unless today is pajama day."

"No," she replied, "I'm not ready, and it's not pajama day. Were you just here a little bit ago?"

"Um, no," he said, "just got here. May I come in?"

"Did you see anyone leaving my apartment when you came up?" Jessi asked.

Jim thought for a moment and then said, "Nope. I don't think I saw anyone at all. Why? What's going on? Are you secretly seeing someone you don't want me to know about?" Jim smiled at his own joke.

"Come in, Jim. Sorry to make you stand out there," Jessi said somberly.

Jim stopped smiling. He suddenly realized this wasn't a joking matter and became concerned.

Jessi continued, "There wasn't supposed to be anyone here at all last night except for me, but when I woke up this morning, I heard a noise. When I came out to investigate, the front door was open, and it looked like it was being closed from the outside."

"That's scary!" Jim said. "Are you okay? Is there anything missing?"

"I'm okay," Jessi replied, "and I don't know if anything is missing. I haven't had a chance to look around yet." She was still in thought when another thought hit her. "Why are you here, Jim?"

"What?" Jim asked.

"Why are you here?" Jessi asked again. "It's like seven in the morning on my sleep-in day."

"Um, you asked me to meet you here at seven so we could get moving. Looks like maybe you stuck to your old habits and slept in any way. Can I take you out and get us some breakfast or something?"

"Breakfast?" Jessi asked, still tired and a little confused. "Wait, wait, wait. I don't remember asking you to come over. When did I do that?"

"At dinner last night. Right after the shrimp, remember?" Jim's brother was a hard person to wake up in the mornings, too, so he was used to this behavior. He actually found it to be a fun game trying to show the sleepy person things they didn't remember and be convincing about it.

Jessi thought and thought, and finally, it hit her. "I'm so sorry. I do remember now. Yes, breakfast. Let me get changed really quick. I'm so sorry. I'll be out in a minute." And with that, she ran down the hallway. No sooner had she reached her bedroom door than another loud crash came from the front room. "Jim, are you trying to destroy my house?" she yelled as she walked back down the hallway. When she arrived at the front room, she saw Jim lying on his back, on the floor, and the front door open again. She ran over to Jim to see if he was okay.

"Jim! What happened?" Jessi helped Jim stand up. He rubbed the back of his head and looked around, walking over to shut the front door.

"I'm fine," he said, arching his back. "Someone ran out from behind the kitchen counter over there, hit me in the face, knocked me down, and ran out the door. I couldn't see who it was, though. It all happened pretty quick and took me by surprise. I hit my head on the floor. I don't think that I'm hurt." He sniffed.

"Let me get you a tissue," Jessi said. "Your nose is bleeding."

Jim reached around and touched under his nose. He looked at his fingers and saw the blood. "I need to sit down," he said. "I don't do well with blood, especially if it's my own."

Jessi helped him to an oversized chair and grabbed a box of tissues from the kitchen. She grabbed a plastic grocery store bag and brought it to him. You can put the tissues in here.

"Thank you, Jess," he said, grabbing a tissue and holding it on his nose.

"Here," Jessi said, grabbing another tissue. "Put this in your nostril." She rolled up the tissue and handed it to Jim, who stuffed it in the bleeding hole. "Now, tip your head back slightly. It will help. I've had plenty of bloody noses."

"Thank you," Jim said. "I can't believe that guy. I don't even know if it was a guy. Just someone who knocked me down and took off running."

"So someone was here and probably waiting for me. It's a good thing you remembered to show up this morning. Before we leave, I'll have the manager change the locks," she said. "In the meantime, do you think you can stay out of trouble long enough for me to change so we can get out of here?"

"Yeah, but aren't you going to call the police?" Jim asked.

"Not now," Jessi shouted as she walked down the hallway to her room. "I'm pretty sure we'll see them later, and I'll try to remember to bring it up then."

"Okay," Jim said. "If you don't mind, I'm just going to lock the door until we leave, though. That gave me the creeps!"

"No argument from me!" Jessi yelled from her bedroom.

She quickly brushed her hair and thought about Jim being in the other room. There was a feeling of safety. No, it wasn't a feeling of safety as much as a feeling of comfort that someone else was here. She never truly felt unsafe alone, but it was nice knowing someone was waiting for her just down the hall.

# CHAPTER 12

## FIRST STEPS

"Thank you for coming so quickly," Jessi told the apartment maintenance man. "I really appreciate you doing this."

"No problem, Jess," he said. "I'm glad you weren't hurt. I'll rekey the lock for you and put in a deadbolt. When you get back, just stop by the office and pick up your new key."

Jim and Jessi walked down the hall toward the entrance.

"Where did you want to go for breakfast?" Jim asked.

"Not sure," Jessi said. "Do you have any ideas?"

"Maybe," Jim said. "Let's get in the car, and I'll surprise you."

Fifteen minutes later, they pulled into the parking lot of one of the best buffet restaurants in town.

"Oh! I love this place," Jessi exclaimed. "I haven't been to a buffet in forever!"

"I thought this would be a good place for breakfast since it allows you to select whatever you want and however much you want! *And* we don't have to wait for the food to come to us since we go to the food!"

"A wonderful idea, my friend," she said, walking through the door.

They didn't talk much about what they would do later in the day. They had a plan and had a little time to just relax. Jessi liked getting to know Jim and enjoyed telling him about herself.

"I was an only child," Jessi said. "My parents and I got along well and had a very special relationship. We still get along better than most!"

"I like that," Jim said between bites of pancake. "I have two brothers and a sister. I'm the youngest of the four. My mom doted over me. My dad was never there. He was always working so that mom could stay home. It was hard because I'd hear stories about how my dad used to always be home and how my brothers and sister would love spending time with him. I always wondered if he had to work so much because I was born. I wondered if my siblings blamed me for Dad not being there. They've never said anything to indicate that, but I still wonder."

Jessi looked at him. "Whatever your dad decided to do or not do wasn't your fault. He did what he did. He had choices. You were young and had nothing to do with his decisions." Jessi thought for a moment. "What does your dad do now?"

Jim was quiet. "Dad died when I was sixteen. I never really had the chance to talk to him about him being gone when I was younger. I talked to Mom about Dad not being around, and she always assured me that it wasn't me, but then, she was my mom. Ever since my dad died, I wanted to make sure that whatever I did, I did it well. I wanted to someday become a father and attentive husband. I believe that will happen someday."

"Of course it will, Jim," Jessi said. "You're a very sweet guy. Take today, for example; you could be doing anything, but you chose to come out early and help me. You don't know me, but you're still willing to help on this crazy chase."

"There's a life at stake, Jess, and not just that, but I *want* to help you. I want to help show others what you can do is real. It's important to me that your ability helps save this life."

Jessi's heart loved hearing what was being said and loved Jim's willingness to help for those reasons. She took another bite of her breakfast and looked at Jim in an entirely different way.

By the time they were ready to leave, they were full, happy, and smiling despite the looming task ahead.

Jessi's cell phone rang in the parking lot on their way to Jim's car. She looked at it and saw that it was Erin.

"Hey Erin," Jessi said, "what's up?"

Erin sounded frantic. "Jess," she said, "I was supposed to meet Barry at his apartment this morning. We talked about this extensively last night. I reminded him when he dropped me off at my place. You know how he can be forgetful sometimes. Before he left, he said he had to head over to his office and work for a few more hours. I reminded him again, and he promised me he would be ready, but he wasn't there when I arrived at his apartment this morning."

"Have you tried calling his cell?"

"I *have* tried calling and it's either off or dead because it goes straight to voicemail. Then I called his work, and they said he wasn't there, so I don't know what else to do."

"Wow! That's crazy. I hope he's okay. Is there anything that we can do to help?"

"I just don't know," Erin said. "I know that we have a lot to do and that you need my help today."

Did you want to meet up with Jim and me?" Jessi asked.

"I want to help with this, Jess, but I'm worried sick about Barry. I think I'm just going to keep trying to find him for a while. I want to make sure he's safe before I kill him for worrying me like this. I'll keep looking for another hour, but I promise to keep you posted."

"Okay, Erin," Jessi said, "I'll keep you updated on where we are too. And don't worry. I'm sure he's fine."

"I hope so," Erin said. "Talk to you later."

Jessi hung up her phone and shook her head.

"What's up?" Jim asked.

"Erin's been trying to find Barry," Jessi explained. "He said he was working late last night but wasn't home when Erin got over to his place this morning. Then she checked his work, and he wasn't there, either. She's tried his cell, but it's turned off."

"Nice summary," Jim whistled. "Maybe he fell asleep somewhere. Like in the bus station or in a taxi. He might be racking up the miles in this city somewhere!"

"Maybe," Jessi said. She looked at her phone. "Okay, so it's eight thirty-five. That means we have seven hours and fifteen minutes to go. We really need to get moving, Jim. We have a lot to get done, and we're not even sure Erin and Barry will be able to help. We might be on our own."

The two hurried out to Jim's car and drove off. The conversation was sparse on the ride to the Channel 7 building but not absent. The conversations they were having in the restaurant continued, to some extent, during the drive.

"So you're the baby of the family, eh?" Jessi asked.

"Yeah. My older siblings are all married, and I'm an uncle four times over. We have a pretty fun family," Jim said, "I think you'd like them. You're pretty lucky, though."

"What do you mean?" Jessi asked.

"Well, I might be the baby of the family, but you're all levels of kid. You're the baby, the middle child, and the oldest. It must be tough on you to be all those kids."

Jessi laughed. She liked how Jim looked at things a little differently than anyone she had ever known. She was about to tell him that when a white panel van sped around Jim and cut in front of him.

"That was rude," Jessi said.

Then the van stopped suddenly. Jim was ready and stopped in time to avoid an accident. The van sped up, but Jim had already decided to keep his distance. Without notice, one of the back doors opened, and a masked individual could be seen standing in the opening. They could see that he was having trouble standing and keeping his balance.

"What is he doing?" Jessi asked.

"Hang on," Jim said. He checked the rearview mirror and saw that it was clear in the next lane but a car was directly behind him. He was about to change lanes when Jessi screamed, "Look out!"

Jim looked ahead and saw the man in the van raising what looked like a long metal pipe. He threw the pipe at the car and quickly closed the van door. Knowing that no one was in the lane coming up next to him, Jim swerved into the left lane just as the pipe hit the back bumper of the car and glanced off. It bounced once and hit the car behind them, exploding and causing the vehicle to swerve and roll, catch fire, and cause the cars behind to screech to a halt.

The van took a sharp right and sped away down a side street.

Jim drove another block and turned into a parking lot, pulling into a parking spot and turning off the car.

"What are you doing?" Jessi asked.

"My knees have turned to jelly, and I need to let them solidify a little before I start to drive again." He took a deep breath. "Jess, do you think what happened to us was just bad luck, or do you think they targeted us?"

"I don't know," Jessi said. "I'm guessing that it was someone who didn't want us to complete what we are doing, but I don't know why they would go to such lengths to stop us."

"I think we need to get to the station and get some investigating going," Jim said. He turned the key and drove out amidst the sounds of sirens coming to the rescue of the people who had been injured.

Jessi worried about saving the woman who would be murdered later in the day. She worried about Barry. She worried about Erin. She worried about whether she would live to see thirty without getting an ulcer from worrying so much.

Jim, on the other hand, was just quiet.

When they arrived in the parking lot, Jim shut off the car and started to get out, but Jessi grabbed his arm, stopping him. "So Jim," she said, "last night you said that your sister-in-law wasn't a reporter."

"Yeah?" Jim said, "That's right."

"I'm curious. You never said what her job is here at the station. What exactly does she do? She's not like a security guard or receptionist or something, is she?"

Jim laughed, "No, not exactly. You'll see. Let's go in."

Jessi's curiosity was piqued more than ever now. She wanted to know, but Jim would obviously not let the secret escape before he was ready.

"This is where the station is?" Jessi asked.

"Yeah, why?"

"I was just down here yesterday morning before work," she said. "I came down to go to that coffee shop across the street." She pointed to Galaxy Coffee.

"Not many people know that the Channel 9 offices are upstairs in this building," Jim said.

They got out of the car, and Jim led the way. When they got to the front doors and entered the lobby area, they saw many people walking to and from the front doors, a desk inside the elaborate lobby, and numerous employees and security guards. Most of them had a badge on, but a few didn't.

Jessi and Jim walked inside and over to the desk, where one of the security guards was sitting. The guard looked up and smiled.

"Well, bless my soul. Hello, Mr. Johnson! How are you today? I haven't seen you in, gosh, how long has it been?" The guard stood up from behind the desk and stuck out his hand. He firmly clasped Jim's hand and gave him a warm and exuberant handshake.

"I'm doing well, Bill, and it's great to see you. How's your family?"

"Oh, you know," Bill said, "the kids are growing more daily, and Julie's expecting again."

"No kidding?" Jim said, "Is this number three for you guys?"

"Yes sir," Bill beamed, "number three it is. You need to stop by sometime. I'll let you know when we have a bar-b-que next time, and you can bring your beautiful lady friend here." The guard looked slightly embarrassed, "But I forget my manners. I'm Bill Wickens."

"Jessi O'Donnell," Jessi said, shaking the guard's hand.

"My, you have quite the grip. Let me guess, you must be a martial artist of some kind."

"Kung Fu," she said, "but how did you know."

"In my line of work, I shake many hands and look into many eyes. You get to know people, both a little about their background and a little about their character. You've got a strong background and a strong character." He looked at Jim, "You need to hold on to this one. She'll be good for you."

Jim looked at Jessi and smiled. "Trying, Bill. Trying."

"So anyway, Mr. Johnson, I'm sorry I got us all sidetracked here. What brings you in today?"

"Well, I was hoping to sneak upstairs and bother Lynette or have her sneak down here so I can chat with her. Any chance of you making that happen for me with your magical charms?" Jim asked.

"I can't be one hundred percent sure," Bill said, picking up the phone, "but you know I'll do my best. Give me just one second."

While the guard was making his call, Jessi pulled Jim aside, and half whispered, "Mr. Johnson? What's up with that? And how is it that you walking into the building is like homecoming week? Bar-b-ques? Family talk? What's this all about?"

"Well," Jim looked down rubbing his neck, "Lyn is well-known here at the station. It never hurts to know people in high places."

"High places?" Jessi questioned. "What do you mean…"

The guard interrupted, "Mrs. Johnson said she's excited you're here and will be down shortly to see you."

"Thanks, Bill," Jim waved as he walked toward the elevator. "Don't forget to say hi to the family for me."

"Don't you forget about the bar-b-que," he told Jim. "Pleasure to meet you, miss."

"You too, Bill!" Jessi waved.

Jessi's curiosity was racing. She wanted to know what made Jim so well known here.

"Jim, just exactly what does your sister-in-law do here?"

Jim walked over to the marquee on the wall next to the large bank of elevators. He looked at Jessi and pointed. She walked over and looked. "Where?" she asked. "I don't see her name."

Jim placed his finger on the glass at the very bottom. Jessi looked again but still didn't see his sister-in-law's name. "What? Where?" Jessi said and looked at Jim, who was smiling at her.

"Follow my finger," he said, moving his finger up the glass. It continued to go up until it reached the top. The very top! The top line read, "Lynette Johnson, RNM." Jessi mouthed the words.

"What is RNM?" she asked.

"Regional Network Manager," Jim said. "That's their fancy term for saying she runs the whole show."

Before Jessi could reply, the elevator made a dinging sound, and the doors of the farthest car came alive. A woman in her early thirties emerged. She was attractively dressed in expensive business attire with shoulder-length brown hair. Her high heels clicked as she stepped out of the elevator and looked around.

Jim held up his arm and waved at her.

She finally saw the waving motion and hurried over, spreading her arms wide and smothered Jim in a big embrace.

"Jimmy!" she said, a little on the loud side. "It's so good to see you! You never come to see your brother and me anymore. Have you become too good for us?" Lyn chuckled at her joke.

"Nah," Jim said. "Just keep forgetting the code to your front gate," Jim chuckled. "I've just been swamped, but I'm sure you know nothing about being busy."

"Oh, you know I do! And who's this with you? New girlfriend? Fiancée?" Lyn gasped, "Is that why you wanted to see me? To bring me some big news?"

"Calm down, Lyn. This is, um, well, uh…"

Jessi took a step forward and stuck out her hand. "I'm Jessi O'Donnell," she said. "Not fiancée and not quite a girlfriend. We've worked together for a long time and just went out together for the first time last night."

There were so many things that Jim wanted to say and ask, all revolving around the last sentence uttered by Jessi, but he thought it would have to wait. He made a mental note to bring it up another time.

Lyn shook Jessi's hand. "It's nice to meet you," she said, "Don't let Jimmy scare you off. Deep down, he's really not a bad guy." Lyn smiled at Jim. "So Jimmy, what brings you here today then? I assume it's not a family matter and apparently not a social call."

Jim thought for a moment. "No. Actually, it's a matter of great importance. Life and death, really. But there's a strange twist that needs to be explained deftly. Is there some private place where we can talk, and how much time do you have?"

"Privacy? In a television station? Ha! You're funny as ever, Jimmy. Come up to my office. It's about as private as you'll get around here. But it's pretty high up, so God might be listening. You don't mind, do you?"

Lyn's face was stone serious, but only for a little bit. Then she burst out laughing. The others laughed with her and followed her into the private elevator. "But Jimmy, this had better be good. We might be family, but I can't just take time off for nonsense."

"Believe me, sis. What I'm about to tell you will make all other stories pale in comparison."

# CHAPTER 13

## BARRY

Erin placed her phone face down on the dining room table, automatically ending the call. She had been trying to reach Barry all morning and didn't know where else to look or call. She walked around her apartment, searching the air for a mysterious answer that didn't seem to reveal itself. She was at her wit's end. She thought about trying his apartment landline again and reached for her phone, but heard a knock at her front door just as she hit the dial icon. She immediately ran to the door and peered out of the peephole. Her initial reactions were relief and joy. She pulled open the door and then threw her arms around Barry. Barry, surprised, didn't know what to do at first but then hugged her back.

In retrospect, he should have just been quiet. But, being the man he was, he opened his mouth. What came out of his mouth should have never done so. "I should get this kind of welcome all of the time!"

The hug would have lasted longer had he just enjoyed the moment. However, the statement acted as a catalyst and sped up the time that Erin's concern warmed her heart. As a result, her heart cooled rapidly, and her fears quickly evolved into the anger that inevitably follows the knowledge that the one you love hasn't died but instead was intentionally not there.

She wriggled out of the embrace that, to Barry, had now lasted less time than he wanted, "Where have you been?" she demanded, smacking him on the chest with the flat of her hand.

"I shouldn't get this kind of welcome anytime," he said, again realizing that his mouth should never open before his brain had a chance to evaluate the situation and come up with a good, sensitive thing to say.

"Barry! I'm serious!" she said, storming into the house, leaving him alone on the porch. He slinked in after her. "I've been trying to reach you all morning, and you haven't been anywhere. Most of all, you haven't answered your phone!"

"I've been somewhere," he replied, "just not where you looked. Why were you trying to get a hold of me?"

"Because it's after nine o'clock, and you're late!" Erin hollered.

"Only a few minutes," he said.

Erin whirled around and stared at him. "A few minutes? A few minutes? A FEW MINUTES? You were supposed to be here at seven this morning!"

Barry needed clarification. He looked at the floor, then back at Erin, then to the floor again. "No," he said, thinking hard, "I'm pretty sure you said to be here at nine. And here I am."

Erin turned and walked across the room, then returned to face Barry again.

"Why haven't you been answering your phone?"

"If it had rung, I would have answered it, but it hasn't made a sound all morning."

"That's funny," Erin said, "cause I've been trying to call it all morning."

Barry reached into his pocket and took out his phone. Without even looking at it, he handed it to Erin. She looked at the screen and pressed the button on the top of the phone. The screen lit up momentarily and with a message and then went dark. Erin shook her head and handed the phone back to Barry.

"You're such a dork!" she said to him. "The battery's dead. When did you charge it last?"

"Well, I thought I plugged it in last night when I got home, but I guess I missed it. I hate it when that happens. Oh well, I can charge it in the car today. But that explains why it's been so quiet." He walked over to Erin. "I'm sorry, honey. I really thought I wasn't supposed to be here until nine. And if I had known the battery was dead, I would have found another way to call you."

The more Barry spoke, the more Erin's anger melted. She gave him a slight smile. "Dork." She said to him.

Barry put his hands on Erin's waist and gave her a kiss. He started to feel a little passionate and kissed her more. She pushed him away and said, "Barry, not now. We need to get going and help Jessi. We're already late."

"Aw, come on," Barry said, "Nothing's going to happen out there," he motioned toward the front door with his head, "for another seven hours. We may as well make something happen in here now. Then we can go out and help in a little while."

"Barry, this is important. We need to get moving and help Jessi!"

"It's important to me that I make it up to you. I need to know that you forgive me," Barry cooed, holding Erin tighter.

"We need to get to the police station," Erin said.

"It's Saturday," Barry said, kissing Erin on the neck. "Most of the detectives take the weekend off." He kissed her again. "The ones that work on the weekend probably don't come in until late morning."

"Barry," Erin's attempt to have him stop was weak, and her resolve was growing weaker by the second. She looked into his puppy dog eyes and sighed, knowing that they wouldn't be leaving for a little while.

# CHAPTER 14

## CONVINCING

The Channel 7 building was one of the tallest in the city, and the elevator ride took a little time.

"Are you okay, Jess?" Jim asked.

"Yeah," she said distractedly. "Why?"

"Well, you've been holding onto my arm for the past thirty seconds or so. Not that I mind, but it's a good grip."

Jessi looked at Jim and noticed a slight smile. "I've never liked elevators. I'm not bothered by the small space, but I just hate the feeling it gives me in the pit of my stomach."

"I've always loved elevators," Jim said, still smiling.

"They make me a little lightheaded, and I'll be happy when we reach whatever floor is our final destination!"

With those words, the elevator slowed, and the doors opened. Jessi released Jim's arm and hurried out into the safety of the hallway.

Lyn and Jim exited. "Are you okay, Jess?" Lyn asked.

"Jessi caught her breath and replied, "Yes. Lead the way." She didn't want to admit it aloud, but her legs were still shaky.

"Good," Lyn said, leading the way the short distance to her office.

"This is much better," Jessi said, entering the office. She whistled. "Very nice! Much nicer than my small office at Thompson's!"

Lyn indicated some chairs around a coffee table. After they sat, Lyn spoke up, "Okay, Jimmy. What's this all about?"

"Well," Jim started, "it's an amazing story and would take a long time to tell, but I know how busy you are, so I'll get right to the point." Although Jim felt comfortable around his sister-in-law, the subject matter he was about to reveal made him feel somewhat unsure. He took a deep breath and said, "We have information that there will be a murder committed today."

Lyn looked at Jim suspiciously. "A murder?" she questioned. "Did you know that, on average, there are about 46 murders committed every day in this country? So I'm sure you're right. I'm also sure, however, that you mean a specific murder somewhere in this town. So, I'll need you to be more specific. Do you know more about this than it will happen?"

"Yes," Jim answered.

"I need to know the same information every reporter will ask. I need to know the who, what, where, when, and why or as close as you can come to answering those. Okay? So, how did you find this out? What is your source?"

Jim and Jessi looked at each other. Jessi seemed slightly worried, but Jim gave her a reassuring look. "As I said, Lyn, it's an amazing story. You've been involved in the television industry long enough to know that there are many unusual things in this world, right?"

"Oh, here we go. Next, you'll tell me that Jessi here is a psychic or clairvoyant, right?" Lyn looked annoyed and sat back in her chair, folding her arms.

"Neither," Jim said.

"Then what is it? Understand, Jimmy, that I have to be a skeptic first and a reporter second. That's how it works. I ask you questions, and you continue to answer until I'm convinced that what you're telling me has some merit. I'm not attacking you or doubting that what you know is the truth, but you must show me that you believe it enough to sway me to form my own belief and make me feel that I can tell anyone with the same surety you have."

"I understand," Jim said. "So be skeptical and ask your questions, then judge the facts I will give you. You've known me many years and know I'm sensible."

Lyn tilted her head and said, "Well...."

"Okay, okay," Jim laughed. "But more sensible than most or at least, more sensible than many."

"Agreed," Lyn said. "But I also know you've logged many more hours at science fiction conventions than normal people. So, in that particular realm of reality, it doesn't come to your rescue in all of this. Especially how you're starting out. Don't make this 'amazing story' something that becomes so fantastic that I can't believe it."

Jessi looked at Jim. "Science fiction conventions? You?"

"Not always, but sometimes. We're getting off track here, and Jessi, you, and I can discuss conventions later. This has nothing to do with science fiction. It's serious and factual. Will you listen with an open mind?"

"The jury is still sitting in the box," Lyn said and waited.

"Okay, here it is. Jessi can hear the sounds of things that will happen. She can't see or feel them, but she can hear them. Only traumatic things. She hasn't been able to do so all her life, but it happened because of a bus accident. More importantly, Lyn. She has never heard these premonitions where they haven't come true!" Jim paused.

"Go on," Lyn said. "That's certainly not all there is to it."

"You're right," Jim said. "Yesterday, when we were at a warehouse in town conducting an appraisal, Jessi heard a woman scream inside the building. Of course, she ran inside to see if she could help. But when no one was there, she realized it would occur in the future. Today!"

Jim waited. That was the story in a nutshell. Jim and Jessi sat on the edge of their chairs, and Lyn remained seated back in hers with her arms folded.

"That's it," Jim said. "Now you know it all. What are your thoughts?"

"Well," Lyn started, "that certainly is interesting and different," Lyn said flatly.

Jessi stood up. She'd heard this tone before, and suddenly, she was back in her kitchen that first morning she knew she could hear the future. The morning her mother thought Jessi had lost her mind. She could almost smell the pancakes and see her mother's face as she sat in the chair across from her.

"Let's go, Jim," she said. "I knew she wouldn't believe us."

"Now, hold on a minute," Lyn said to Jessi. "Sit back down. You all asked me not to judge, but now you're the one ready to leave. Are you afraid I'll find out the truth?"

"I'm afraid you won't believe the truth. Very few people do," Jessi grumbled.

"Sit down for a moment longer, please." Lyn looked at Jim. "Jimmy? You know me. Tell her."

"Sit down, Jessi," Jim said. If I know Lyn, she's digesting the whole thing. Don't dismiss her yet."

Jessi sat down slowly and looked from Jim to Lyn, waiting for the next words.

"Jimmy," Lyn started, "you know me pretty well." She turned to Jessi and said, "Jessi, I've been involved in television for many years. I started as a reporter and researcher, and I've seen things much more strange than what Jimmy described."

Jim said, "You should hear some of the stories she can tell. I remember this one about…"

Lyn raised her hands. "Jim. Another time. This is important."

Jim stopped talking and sat back. He knew that Lyn was about to read the verdict on the trial.

"Jessi," she said, "how long have you had this ability?"

"About six years," Jessi said.

"And, to your knowledge, has it always been correct?"

"Yeah."

"Is there anything else that you have noticed that would set you apart from others? Some other special ability?" Lyn asked.

"Not that I know of," Jessi said, thinking about it, "but then I'm not sure I understand your question completely. Other abilities like…?"

"Now I'm going to turn the tables a little on you," Lyn said. "I'm sure that when you tell someone about what you can do, you think they will find it strange. What I'm about to tell you might sound different, but I've heard of someone with your ability. It was part of a story I was working on long ago."

Lyn got up and walked over to a filing cabinet near her desk. She opened one of the drawers and began searching through some folders while she continued talking.

"A young girl could hear things that would happen in the future. She had to be at the location, and it was only violent or emotional events."

"That sounds much like what happens to me," Jessi said.

Lyn stopped at a file and said, "Ah, here it is!"

Lyn walked back over to Jessi and handed her the file. Jim moved his chair closer to look as well.

Lyn kept talking, "Anyway, the girl's name was Marla, and she received all sorts of flack about her ability. Hearing the future sounds wasn't the only thing she noticed being able to do. She found that she acquired other abilities as well. She could sense certain things, almost like a psychic."

"What do you mean?" Jessi asked, glancing up from the file.

"Whenever she spoke to people, she could tell if they were telling the truth or lying. More remarkably, she could tell to what extent that person was lying. She was like a human lie detector. It was extremely disconcerting to many people."

"That's interesting." Jessi continued scanning through the papers. "Since you mention it, though, I find certain people distasteful. When I was younger, before the accident, I loved everyone."

"Marla's went a little bit further than that, I think. She could judge a person's character. In other words, she could tell by meeting you if you were good or evil."

"Wow!" Jessi looked distant. "I thought I had it bad. I should consider myself lucky to only have the hearing thing going on. So whatever happened to Marla?"

Lyn looked down at the floor. "She died. A very violent death actually, at the hand of a killer who had set her up."

"Set her up?" Jessi asked.

"He lured her to the place where he tortured and killed her. It was an unfortunate case. She was such a sweet girl."

"Did they catch her killer?"

"That's the saddest part. They never did. It's a cold case now. I know that the police look at varying leads occasionally, but when they're tracking a serial killer like they are now, they really don't have time to keep officers working the cold cases."

"How did she die?" Jessi wondered out loud.

"She was stabbed twenty-seven times. The coroner said that she had been tortured first. It was a pretty nasty scene for all involved. But I think we've discussed Marla too long. Let's talk about your situation."

"My situation? You mean the murder I heard?"

"I want to know more about the murder, yes, but I want to know if there is anything that you can do to convince me that your ability is real. In other words, you're about to tell me about a murder. That's a very serious crime and will take a lot of convincing and me pulling in a lot of favors to investigate this quickly. So, is there something that you can provide me as solid proof? Something to show me your ability is real? It's not that I'm doubting you. I just need something to pass along to say that I've seen this work. Do you have anything?"

Jessi thought but felt a sudden defeat. She had no idea what she could come up with. She had never thought of documenting what she heard. She searched, and she thought, and then it hit her. She stood up, reached into the front pocket of her jeans, and fished out a few wrinkled pieces of paper. "What time is it?"

Jim looked at his phone and said, "Nine twenty-one. Why?"

She looked at paper after paper and then stopped. She held up one piece and said, "This is it." She had a receipt and searched for the time. When she found it, she said, "Nine twenty-three."

"What are you talking about, Jess?" Jim asked.

Wild-eyed, Jessi looked at Lyn, "I was across the street yesterday at the coffee shop. I got my coffee at nine twenty-three. A few minutes later, I heard a plane crash. From what I could hear, the plane flew really low to these buildings and landed hard a few blocks away. You should have a good view from up here. If that happens, will that be proof enough?"

"Let's go to the window," Lyn said, and the three went quickly to the glass that allowed them to overlook the city. "How long after you got your coffee did this happen?" Lyn asked, checking her watch.

"It wasn't that long," Jessi said, staring out the window.

The three were quiet, anticipating the event. Not a sound. No plane. They waited.

Jessi's anxiousness started to melt into fear. She was suddenly afraid that nothing was going to happen.

Lyn took a deep breath and was about to say something when the windows shook. The roar of the airplane engine went from a distant hum to a loud, rumbling, and low sound in moments. The plane's wings came uncomfortably close to the glass as it passed by the window and cruised by, losing altitude more every second. They watched as it descended rapidly and hit a distant park field. It was still early enough that the local soccer players hadn't arrived yet, and it seemed no one was hurt.

The three stood quietly at the window, trying to understand what they had just seen. Lyn held the deep breath she had taken and slowly let it out. She turned to Jessi.

"Well," she said, "I didn't expect such an impressive and emotional demonstration of your ability. You've left no doubt in my mind that your ability is real. Let's sit back down."

They walked over and sat back in their chairs.

"So you believe us?" Jim asked.

"Yes," Lyn said. "Where and when?"

"What?" Jessi asked.

"Your murder. Where will it happen and when?"

"The scream I heard will occur at three-fifty this afternoon at the empty warehouse just off Crossroads Blvd."

Lyn looked up at her clock. "Okay. It's nine-thirty now, giving us about six and a half hours. I'll make a few calls and see if I can get someone out there. I don't want you two going out there. Do you understand? It will be too dangerous."

"But Lyn," Jim whined, "I want to see what's going to happen. I'm sure Jessi wants to see as well."

"Jimmy," she said, sounding more like a mother than a sister-in-law, "This is serious. Don't mess with it. I'll call you if things change. I have your cell number, even if I don't use it often. Going out there will just make things worse. At the very least, you'll get in the way. I don't want to think about what could happen beyond that."

Jim sat next to Jessi and pouted. "Okay," he said, more like a hurt child.

"Thank you for your help," Jessi said, standing and reaching to shake Lyn's hand.

"Yeah. Thanks, Lyn." Jim said.

"Thanks to both of you," Lyn said, shaking Jessi's hand. "I'll do everything I can to help. Remember, though, do not, I repeat, *do not*, go out there. Let me take care of things. You two should just go home and relax. Do you understand me, Jimmy?"

Jim looked at Lyn. "I understand," he said. But even though he understood, he wasn't sure they could comply.

# CHAPTER 15

## CONVINCING BARRY

Erin walked out of her bedroom. She wasn't happy, and even though she loved being with Barry, there was something off about him lately. Today, it was beginning to get under her skin. She knew how important it was to help Jessi, and she felt in her heart that Barry either couldn't grasp that fact or he didn't care. Jessi had been her best friend for years. Much longer than she had known Barry. She hoped she and Jessi would remain friends for the rest of their lives. They were like sisters. They shared so much, and it went deeper than just a friendship. She never really knew how to describe it, but she knew Jessi felt it, too.

Erin walked to the front door, put her hand on the knob, her forehead on the door, and her heart on hold. Barry walked up behind her, wrapped his arms around her, and kissed her neck. Where she usually would love this attention, she wanted to turn and push him away right now. *What is wrong with him*, she thought. *Why can't he just be compassionate instead of passionate?*

"Please stop," Erin said. When he continued kissing her neck, she said, "Barry, we should go," and shrugged from under his grip.

"It was wonderful," was his reply. "You are wonderful."

"Uh-huh." Erin didn't know what to say.

Even though he continued to hold her, she felt Barry's physical hold on her change. "What's wrong?" he asked and, for the first time, looked concerned.

"Nothing. I am just feeling a little weird right now. It must just be the situation and all. Knowing that someone's going to get killed and I should be out there helping to stop it, with you by my side as you promised."

"I understand, Hun," he said, tightening his hug around her again. "Maybe we should go out and grab a bite to eat. There's this new restaurant that just opened down the street. We could grab lunch and then head to the police station."

Erin looked up and glared at him. She took a short step toward him, ending up nose to nose. The sudden movement startled Barry and caused him to let go of her. He took a small step back.

"Something to eat?" she questioned. "You feel that now, after a long and wasted morning, we should go out and get something to eat? Is that what you're telling me?"

"Yeah," he said. "We need to keep up our strength, ya know. And we don't have to rush over there right now. They'll still be there in an hour or so. Besides, I'm starving! And I don't know about you, but I'm not so eager to rush down to the police station with this story. How do you think they'll take it? I should have just listened to everyone else about this idea."

"Why does it seem like you're trying to delay this whole thing?" Erin was getting mad. "It was your idea to begin with and stupid or not, we said we would do it. We owe this to Jessi. You need to keep your word, like it or not."

"I know, I know," Barry said, holding his hands in front of him. "Just don't fault me for wanting to spend a little time with my girl."

"I don't fault you for that, you goof. However, it would help if you listened to me. You made a promise to help with this. If you don't keep this promise, I'm not sure I can ever trust any of your promises. We promised, and I want to help my friend and prevent someone from losing their life. How would you feel seeing her in the paper, knowing her name and that she was dead and you didn't do *anything* to stop it, even though you promised to do it? What if it were me you were reading about? How would you feel then, Barry?"

Barry's eyes became wide as saucers. "You're right. I didn't think about that. I guess this person could be someone's girlfriend. Let's get going and at least try. Let's go."

Erin smiled. Barry opened the door and let Erin go first. Turning to close the door, he took one last lingering look inside the apartment and smiled at the thought of them being together.

# CHAPTER 16

## THE POLICE

Erin was a little more than nervous with what they were about to do. She has friends who used to work for the police and others who still do but now work in other towns for other departments. She thought that maybe she should have tried calling them first, but then realized that she hadn't spoken with them in almost a year. Barry was quiet. Erin spoke up.

"Barry, what are we going to say to the police? Have you thought about how we're going to present this?"

"No," Barry said flatly and continued to look at the road.

Erin wasn't sure what Barry meant by that and why he wouldn't look at her. Was he still angry? "Do you want *me* to talk to the police? I will if you want to just wait in the car."

"I'll talk to them," Barry said. "I'm unsure what to say, but I'll think of something. You were right, and I'm sorry, babe. I made a promise, and I'm sorry I let you down."

Erin started feeling bad. "You didn't let me down, Barry. I just wish that we had started this earlier. The good thing is that we're on our way and still have time. I'm just worried about what we'll say and how it will be received. We need the police to help, and I don't want to blow it."

Barry was silent. "I'm worried, too, but we'll figure something out and save this girl."

Erin started to remember why she liked this man. There was a side of him that she wanted at the beginning, and even though that side had been hiding for some time, it was now peeking out slightly. She loved that, and it made her smile just a bit, and then a bit more.

When they arrived, they parked in the lot and walked a short distance to the front entrance of the police station. There were two sets of glass doors that they had to pass through, and Barry wondered if he was being scanned or videotaped as he walked in. He felt the childish urge to make some faces but then was afraid Erin would catch him and be mad again.

"You know they are probably videotaping us," he said to Erin.

"Probably," she said. "It's the police department."

"I hate when people video me. What if they make fun of me later on? What if they use the video to get laughs at their Christmas party?"

Erin stopped, sighed, and turned to Barry. "Why would they do that, and honestly, who cares? Neither of us will be there, and no matter what they do or view at their party, we won't know about it."

"That's what bothers me."

"Sometimes you're unbelievable," she said, shaking her head. She turned and started walking again, leaving Barry bewildered.

Barry had always been slightly paranoid when it came to the police. He wasn't sure why, but still, the paranoia was there. He didn't feel comfortable walking through the second set of doors.

Barry placed a hand on Erin's shoulder.

"What now, Barry?"

"I think those officers over there are looking at us," he said, nodding toward the officers at the desk.

"We just walked in!" Eric said quietly but forcefully. "Of course they're looking at us."

"What if I get arrested?"

"Why would that happen? Why are you so paranoid?"

"I don't know," he replied. "I've always been a little scared of authorities and afraid I'll get stopped and arrested for something I didn't do. I hope it never happens, but now I feel like I'm walking into the lion's den."

"We're walking into someplace for help. Keep that in the forefront of your mind," Erin said.

They walked across the almost empty lobby to a high desk. Two uniformed officers sat behind the desk at either end. Barry motioned for Erin to stay back. "I'll be the brave one. I'll go up and talk to them and see what we need to do," he said.

Oddly, what Barry was doing seemed logical to Erin. She thought that his taking the lead and wanting to ask the questions was something that he should naturally do. Then, she thought about the fact that this was Barry. She loved him but realized he wasn't always the brightest bulb in the chandelier. She didn't want to think too hard about it as she might get upset with him again. It seemed to happen a lot whenever she thought too hard about Barry.

She watched Barry walk up to the desk and then as he was talking with the female officer on the left. He spoke so low that Erin couldn't hear what was being said. She thought about going up, but then the officer pointed at her. The mere act of the officer pointing at her made her feel incredibly uncomfortable. Barry turned, looked at her, and waved. Then he turned back to the officer and nodded. *What are they talking about?* Erin thought to herself. As if hearing her thoughts, the officer looked up again at Erin. She didn't look happy. In fact, her look made Erin more than uncomfortable. It made her a little nervous. She really didn't want to be anxious in a police station, and she had always been told that there was no reason to be shy around the police. But, except for her friends, it seemed that the only time she encountered a police officer was when she was in trouble, like being pulled over. She took a deep, slow breath and tried to be calm, but somewhere in her mind, she had to wonder if she had an unpaid parking ticket floating around somewhere.

When she looked back up at the desk, two more officers stood behind the first one. The female officer spoke to them and pointed at Erin. Erin felt very vulnerable standing in the large, open lobby by herself. The two new officers walked to the back, behind the desk, and disappeared. They emerged from a side door a moment later and walked over to Erin. Barry walked over to meet them. If she was nervous about things before, her mind took her to places she didn't want to visit now. Why were two officers coming over? She should have gone to the desk with Barry. She swallowed hard and forced a smile.

Both officers were male and were in perfect shape. The first officer approached Erin. She noticed he wore a name tag that read, "Jeffers."

Officer Jeffers stopped in front of Erin and said, "Would you come with us, please?"

"Of course," she said to the officer. She turned to Barry and whispered, "Could you tell me what's happening?"

"Oh, they just want to talk to us briefly."

"For a little bit? What did you tell them? Are they going to talk to us about what's going on?"

"Yeah," Barry said. "Why else would they be talking to us? Unless you've done something wrong that you haven't told me about. Maybe they did a quick background check and found something on you."

Erin looked at him, her mouth open.

"Kidding," he said.

"Not funny," she snapped back.

Officer Jeffers sighed. "If you please come with us, Detective O'Malley would like to speak with you. This way, please."

"At least they're taking us to see a detective," Erin said.

"I told you that I'd take care of things. We'll just tell him about everything and let the police handle it from there. We go home, and all's right with the world."

"Yeah. I'm sure that's how it's going to work." Erin was doubtful.

Officer Jeffers led the way, and the quiet officer flanked them. They walked through a doorway and, after a few twists and turns, found themselves walking down a long hallway with offices on either side. Barry had grabbed Erin's arm, and as they walked, his grip became tighter and tighter. She finally reached a level of discomfort and pulled her arm away. He tried to grab her arm again repeatedly, but each time she pulled it away. The final time, however, she stopped and faced him.

"What is your problem?" she asked.

"What are you talking about?" Barry asked.

"Why are you grabbing my arm like that?"

"I don't know what you're talking about."

Erin had reached the point where she had enough. "Tell you what, Barry. Don't touch me."

Both police officers had stopped and were looking at the couple.

Officer Jeffers asked, "Do you two want to speak with the detective? If you do, you need to stop fighting and bickering." He looked at Barry and said, "And unless you want to be arrested and charged with domestic violence, I suggest you leave her alone. If she complains again about you touching her, I might have to arrest you for assault."

Barry dropped his head and mumbled something that sounded like he was sorry.

Erin walked to Officer Jeffers and walked next to him.

They continued down the long hallway until they reached almost the last office. Officer Jeffers stopped and said, "This is the detective's office." He let Erin and Barry go in first, and Jeffers followed them. He walked over to O'Malley and whispered something. O'Malley's bushy eyebrows raised, and he glanced at the two people in his office.

"Okay. Thanks, Tom," he said to Jeffers. "Would you mind hanging out outside the door for a few minutes so you can take them back to the front when we're done? If it will take long, I'll let you know."

Detective O'Malley was a career officer. He was promoted to detective six years earlier. He looked older than his 43-year-old with his graying, bushy eyebrows and thinning hair. His desk had piles of paperwork on it. He looked and felt tired. He attempted a smile and looked at Barry and Erin. "Please have a seat. I'll be with you in a moment. Just let me clear away some of this paperwork."

Erin grabbed one of the chairs and moved it close to the wall and away from the second chair on the same side of O'Malley's desk. She plopped down, still angry with Barry.

Barry picked up the other chair, moved it beside her, and sat down.

O'Malley tried to arrange some of the scattered paperwork into not-so-scattered piles, but it is evident that he was just frustrating himself, so he just pushed the semi-piles off to a corner. He reached into his desk drawer and brought a notepad and a pencil.

Half rising from behind his desk, he extended his hand and said, "I'm Detective O'Malley." His hand was met with a very limp handshake from Barry, who murmured his name. O'Malley said, "Excuse me? I didn't quite catch that."

"Sorry," Barry cleared his throat. "Barry. My name is Barry."

O'Malley reached to shake Erin's hand. "I'm Erin," she said.

O'Malley sat back down, folded his hands before him, and looked at the uncomfortable duo. "Before we start, I want you to know and acknowledge that we are being recorded on video. Are you both okay with this?"

Erin nodded.

Barry started looking around the office until he saw the camera. He smiled and waved and ran his fingers through his hair.

O'Malley sighed. "I'll take that as a yes," he said with a sour look. "So, I understand you have some things of importance that you'd like to discuss. How can I help?"

The room was intensely quiet for the first ten seconds. Barry looked at Erin, who looked back at him, each waiting for the other to say something.

Finally, O'Malley let out a big sigh. "Look, folks, I don't have time to sit with you two and play googly eyes all day. If the two of you are mad at each other and just need someone to talk with, counseling is the next block over. If you're here to talk about the details of a crime, I'm the man to talk to right now. And I do mean *right now*. If you haven't noticed, I have a great deal of work on my desk to finish, and I would love for that to happen sometime before midnight. So, Is there something you want to say, or are you leaving?"

"Sorry, sir," Barry spoke up. "My girlfriend and I have some information about a possible murder."

O'Malley leaned forward. "You have just used two words in the same sentence I don't like to hear, Barry. Do you know what those two words are?"

Barry shook his head.

"Those two words, Barry, are 'possible' and 'murder.' Murder is not a nice word around here and greatly concerns us. So please tell me what you know about this."

Again, silence filled the room. O'Malley looked back and forth between the two of them. Finally, his eyes rested on Erin, and he said louder and not-so-nice, "Well?"

"Well, sir, it was actually a friend of mine who said that she had some information about a murder that is supposed to happen this afternoon. We're just trying to find someone to help us prevent that from happening." Erin was still trying to figure out how to tell him without sounding totally and completely insane.

"Uh huh," O'Malley said, rubbing his eyes. "And does this friend of yours have a name?"

"Of course, my friend has a name. What does that matter?"

"The facts, ma'am. I just need the facts." O'Malley chuckled to himself and then looked at Erin. "I've always wanted to have the chance to say that to someone." He knew he needed some sleep. When no one else laughed at his joke, he said, "So you two are serious?"

"Yes, we're serious!" Erin exclaimed. "Can someone come to the warehouse this afternoon to help stop this?"

"Warehouse?" O'Malley said, "Now we're starting to get somewhere. What warehouse are you talking about? Where is this warehouse? Who owns it?"

"There's an empty warehouse out off of Crossroads Boulevard. A woman is going to be murdered there this afternoon." The more Erin said, the crazier it sounded to her.

"A woman?" O'Malley said. "Do you have a name for this woman?"

"No, I don't know who she is, just that she'll be murdered."

"Do you know where she's being held now? At the warehouse, maybe?"

"I," Erin felt as if she were trapped in a game, "I don't know where she is right now. I just know that the murder will occur at three-fifty today."

"I see," O'Malley said, placing his pencil on the desk. "Three-fifty today." The words were measured and spoken slowly. "Your friend told you there will be a murder at this warehouse at three-fifty today?"

Erin nodded.

"But she didn't tell you who?"

Erin shook her head.

"Now, I'm going to ask you another question. This is a fundamental question, and I'll need a frank and straightforward answer. How is it that your friend knows that this will happen?"

"She, um, overheard something about it," Erin said, feeling her face getting red.

"And who did she overhear saying this? Where did this conversation take place?" O'Malley asked patiently.

Barry raised his hand, "Can I say something here?"

Erin felt her stomach knot. She knew that if Batty said anything about what was happening, they would likely be kicked out or put in jail. "He's not talking to you, Barry!" Erin said through clenched teeth.

"Actually," O'Malley said, "I'm talking to both of you. And if it will help us get to the bottom of this before I die, then yes, Barry, please say something."

"Yeah, and thank you, detective!" Barry glanced over at Erin and gave her a smug look. He wanted to stick his tongue out at Erin, but he didn't. Instead, he looked Detective O'Malley straight in the eye and said, "Erin's friend hears things that haven't happened yet, and she heard the woman being murdered yesterday. That's how we know that it's going to happen today."

# CHAPTER 17

## O'MALLEY

O'Malley's mouth could not have dropped open any farther or faster than it did. He stared at Barry for what seemed to be the longest time before sitting back in his chair and rubbing his face in his hands. He was saying something in his hands shallowly, but neither Erin nor Barry could hear precisely what it was. Eventually, he sat back up in his chair and looked again at Barry. He opened his mouth and then closed it. He looked at Erin and asked, "I'm going to assume you're the sensible one on that side of the desk. I've had a long day, which had been preceded by a very long career, so please understand that this next question comes directly from the bottom of my heart," O'Malley took a deep breath and then asked, "Is he serious?"

Erin sat quietly, looking at the ground. She could feel O'Malley's eyes staring at her, waiting for an answer.

"Of course I'm serious!" Barry said, not waiting for Erin to answer. "Why would we take our valuable time to come down and talk to you about this if we weren't serious?"

"Oh, for Pete's sake!" Now O'Malley was turning red. He stood behind his desk and said quietly but with authority, "Get out. Get out of my office." He pointed toward the door.

Barry shrugged, stood, and started toward the door. "C'mon, babe. We tried."

Erin stood but then took a step toward O'Malley's desk. "You've got to believe me! There is going to be a murder. You've got to help us. I understand that my boyfriend, Barry, is sometimes not the most tactful and not the best at explaining things, but he's honest. There is going to be a murder, and we're here begging for you to help us stop it."

"Based on a sound that hasn't happened yet?" he said. "Wait. I'm hearing a sound. The sound of a jail cell door closing soon, with the two of you inside the cell if you don't leave right now."

With tears in her eyes, Erin pushed past Barry and ran out into the hallway. Barry stopped at the door and turned to face O'Malley. "Thank you for taking the time to see us. I apologize for…"

"*Out!*" O'Malley yelled.

Barry rushed to the door where Officer Jeffers was waiting. Jeffers poked his head inside. "Everything okay?"

"Fine. Just fine. Get those crazy people out of this station."

The two were escorted back down the long hallway. Neither Erin nor Barry said a word. Erin continued to wipe away the tears. She felt like she let her friend down. She didn't know what to think about Barry. Officer Jeffers led them to the lobby and showed them to the front door. As they were going through the door, the mailman was just entering and walked over to the desk, where he delivered a bundle of mail.

In the parking lot, Erin was well ahead of Barry. As upset as she was about letting Jessi down, she was now angry at Barry and was storming out to the car and ignoring him calling her. When he finally reached her, he grabbed her arm and turned her around.

"Erin? What's wrong? We tried, and that's all we could do."

Erin glared at Barry, pulled out of his grip, and wiped the few tears from her eyes. "I can't believe you. I just can't believe you at all. What is wrong with you today?"

"I don't know," Barry said, "I guess this whole hanging out at the police station thing made me nervous."

"No, Barry," she said with more tears, "it's been more than that. First, I couldn't get a hold of you this morning, then this whole delaying-the-day thing, and now you're telling the detective all about Jessi by just blurting it out. I don't know what to think. You've been so different lately and have no explanation for it. Things are wrong, and you always seem to have the perfect answer. At least, it's perfect for me. What's going on?"

Barry looked into her eyes and said, "I thought we needed to tell him the truth. I don't want to get in trouble."

"In trouble for what? What do you think they have on you? What have you been doing that you don't want them to know about? No, wait. Let me guess. Unpaid parking tickets?"

"Something like that. Yeah, okay, I don't want the police snooping around right now in my life. Okay?"

"You don't want them snooping around in your life right now, but it's okay to trade that for a woman's life. Is that what you're saying?"

"Erin, baby, you know I'm not saying that," Barry said, reaching for Erin again.

Again, Erin pulled away, still angry. "How do I know that, Barry? How do I know that you're not saying that? I'm not sure that I know what you're saying anymore. I'm not sure that I know who you are anymore. It all seems to revolve around you, Barry. There is just too much that I don't know about you anymore, which bothers me. There are too many secrets, Barry, and I can't live in a relationship where secrets are the priority."

"So, what are you saying?" Barry asked.

"I'm simply saying I want you to be honest and open. You need to include me in what's going on in your life, especially when it's going to affect what's going on in my life."

Barry thought for a moment. "Do you want to talk about it now?" he asked.

Erin sighed. "We'll talk about it later. Let's get in the car and start driving. I'll call Jessi and see how she's doing and fill her in on our disaster. I hope they've been able to make some progress."

Erin opened her door and shot Barry a dirty look as she angrily plopped herself into the passenger's seat, slamming the door.

Barry shrugged, hopped into his side, and pulled out of the parking lot.

At the police station, the officer at the front desk was going through the mail and stopped at one particular letter. The calligraphy on the front was all too familiar. She picked up the desk phone and pushed a button. "Captain? This is Officer Stevens," she said into the phone.

"Yes, Stevens, what can I do for you?"

"Another one just came in, sir."

"Get it to the briefing room right away. We're having a meeting about that right now." The Captain hung up the phone and looked at the officers in the room. "We just received another one. They're bringing it here now. Clear your tablets or go to the section with your previous notes and ideas."

A few minutes later, the letter was being carefully examined. There were officers from every department. Some were going over notes and maps. Others were taking phone calls and sitting at a table waiting to hear what the letter's contents had to reveal. Everyone was tense. They needed to catch this killer, and so far, they were always just a step or two behind him.

"I hate that he's taunting us like this," the Captain said while pacing. "We need to catch this guy and get him off the streets."

Officer Nelson spoke up. "What's in the letter this time?"

The Captain put on his reading glasses and looked at the report he had just handed him. "He says that we'll find another dead victim tonight. Unlike the other letters he sent us, there are no clues about where we will find the body."

"So he just says that we'll find a body tonight? What has changed? What happened to his cryptic clues?"

"In the letter, he says that we have already been told," the Captain said. He thought momentarily and said, "I don't understand how we've already been told. Who told us?"

"Was there a letter that we missed?" another officer asked.

"As far as we know, no other letters have come in. We've diligently screened all the mail, letters, and packages without the calligraphy. Usually, he at least sends some kind of clue just to make us run in circles, but this time is different. All we know from this one is that he's planning another murder today. Something has changed."

As the Captain uttered this statement, O'Malley was walking by the door to the conference room. He stopped when he heard the Captain's words and stuck his head in the room. He wanted to be the man who broke the case open and caught the killer. He needed something like this to go out in a blaze of glory. He didn't have much more time with the department before retirement and wanted his last few years to matter.

"Another murder today? Is this about our serial killer?" he asked. "I just had a couple of loonies in my office talking about a murder that's supposedly going to happen today."

The activity in the room stopped, and all eyes turned toward O'Malley. He suddenly felt like his head had exploded, and no one in the room could believe what they saw.

The Captain yelled, "Get in here!"

O'Malley timidly stepped into the room. "Okay. Was it something I said?"

The Captain looked strained. "Blue Mountain sent us another letter. In it, he says there will be another murder today, that we'll find the body tonight, and that we should already know about it. He said that we've already been told. Who were these 'loonies' that came into your office? What did they look like? Where do they live? I want everything you've got on them. How long ago did they leave?"

O'Malley felt his face flush. "Uh, I only know their first names. They were talking crazy. They had no real leads and no substantiating evidence. They were talking nonsense, Captain. They were talking crazy, so I told them to leave my office and had them escorted out of the building."

"You what?" the Captain bellowed.

"I swear, I thought they were just wasting my time, Captain. They were saying something about hearing about the murder when it hadn't happened yet or that they had a friend who had heard the murder before it was going to happen. I had never heard of such a thing, and we only consider serious leads."

The Captain ran his fingers through his hair and rubbed his face. He was tired and frustrated and realized he couldn't take it out on this man. He took a deep breath and clapped his hand on O'Malley's shoulder. He spoke a little softer. "O'Malley, we have a serial killer running around this town. Every lead, and I mean *every* lead, is to be taken seriously. Where were you during our briefing on this?"

"I, uh, was in that meeting, sir. But this was just crazy. No one can hear something before it happens." O'Malley was trying to help the Captain see why he let these people go. "When they came in, they were fighting with each other. It's more like bickering, really, like boyfriend and girlfriend. I was up to my eyeballs in paperwork, and then they started spouting off about a friend they had who could hear the sounds of things before they happened. Not even see them but only listen to them.

"You were at the briefing, but your brain slept during it." The Captain said. "Okay, let's back up a bit. When did these people come in?"

"They actually just left a few minutes ago," O'Malley said.

"*What?*" The Captain looked frantically around the room. "Why are you just standing there? Go get them! Maybe they're still in the parking lot. Terrence, go check the cameras monitoring the lots. The rest of you come with O'Malley and me. Let's see if we can spot them before they get away."

During the next few minutes, the activity at the station reflected an emergency. Both plain-clothed and uniformed officers poured out the front door, splitting up and running to the parking lots. They were to set up a human roadblock, check any cars leaving, and radio O'Malley for an ID. The Captain and O'Malley stood outside, several feet from the front door, looking around. O'Malley watched some cars driving by on the road in front of the station. He saw a red Toyota Celica going by with Barry at the wheel, and Erin on the phone in the passenger's seat. He pointed to the car and yelled, "That's them." He strained to see the license plate and got a partial. He felt somewhat relieved that he was able to get something. Maybe this tiny act was enough to redeem himself.

The officers were called back to the conference room and gathered into the group of chairs that filled part of the strategy room. The Captain walked to the front of the room and stood at a podium. He grabbed a few papers from a nearby desk and scrawled some notes.

O'Malley wrote down the partial plate number, handing it to the Captain. "Good work, O'Malley," he said, giving the note to a nearby Sergeant. He quickly walked to a new officer, instructed him to take it to the radio room, and put out an all-points bulletin to detain the car's driver and notify the Captain. The officer left immediately, and the rest of the team started working on finding the car and the rest of the license plate number.

The Captain pulled O'Malley aside. "We'll discuss this whole thing later in private. But for now, I want you out there to help us find this car. You had the first contact, and I want you to find out what they know. We have a murder to stop; for all we know, they might be the only clue to stopping it."

"Yes sir," O'Malley said. He left the conference room and went to his office to pick up a few things before he left. He wondered to himself if this wild goose chase was worth it and then what would happen if it turned out to be worth it. He grabbed his hat, ensured he had his gun and badge, and headed out to get a car. He looked in the lot, and all he could find was one of the older, plain cars. He sighed to himself, "Maybe it's a good sign."

# CHAPTER 18

## LUNCH

Jim and Jessi tried to decide what to do next. They both felt good about meeting with Lyn but wondered if it would be enough and in time. They were in the elevator, on their way down to the lobby, and talking as fast as their mouths would allow.

"I can't believe that she believed us," Jessi said.

"That little demonstration you gave certainly didn't hurt," Jim chuckled. "I have to admit that it made me a little nervous when nothing happened at first, but when that plane flew by and almost hit the window, there was no doubt left."

Jessi laughed, "I had no idea it would come so close to the building. I guess that's why so many people were yelling. It's weird to see it happen but not hear what I heard yesterday."

The elevator doors opened, and they stepped out into the lobby. Jessi stopped and turned to Jim. "Thank you," she said.

"For what?" he asked.

"For setting this up with your sister-in-law, but mostly for believing in me."

Jim laughed. "Why wouldn't I believe in you? You're a good, kind, honest person. I can't imagine you lying about anything." Jim started to lose himself in Jessi's eyes. "And the fact that you're really pretty doesn't hurt either."

They both had that feeling, you know, the feeling that you get in your stomach when you know that the time is right and the feeling is mutual and all that, and you're about to share that first kiss. Their eyes started to close, the world began to fade away, and they started leaning in when Jessi's phone rang.

Jessi had forgotten that the phone was in her hand. She felt the blood rush to her face in embarrassment, and she stepped back as she looked at the phone. "It's Erin," she told Jim and answered the phone. "Erin, what's up? How are things going?"

"Oh, Jessi," Erin said. "The trip to the police station was a disaster."

"What happened?"

Jim glanced over at Jessi. He was curious to know what was being said but resigned himself to the fact that he would have to wait and glean what he could from this one side of the conversation.

"We met with this detective, and I think we had his interest until Barry blurted out that we knew about the murder today because you heard it happening yesterday."

"What?" Jessi felt the blood drain from her face. "Why would he do that?"

"I don't know," Erin said. "I don't know why he's doing half the things he's doing today."

Jessi could hear Barry protesting in the background. Erin's cell phone made him sound garbled, but Jessi could pick up every few words and knew what he said wasn't helping his case.

"Did he tell them my name?" Jessi asked.

"I don't think so," Erin said. "I don't remember. I know the Detective asked me, and I don't think I said anything, but the morning is blurred. I was angry at Barry right after we arrived at the police station, so many of my thoughts were tied up. I know that you know what I mean. Barry just kind of took over everything there. I'm so sorry, Jessi."

"So, are the police going to do anything?"

"No," Erin said. "The only action we saw was Barry and I getting kicked out of the detective's office. I thought we would get arrested for wasting time in the first degree. I certainly hope that I never run into that guy again. He actually had us escorted out of the station."

"It's okay, Erin," Jessi said. "Maybe we should all meet for lunch and

112

discuss what, if anything, we can do next. Are you up for lunch or at least something to drink? I'm starving."

"Okay. Think of someplace and give me a call. We'll meet you there." Erin hung up the phone.

Jessi ended her call and turned to Jim.

"Let's head out to the car," Jim said. "We'll get going. I heard you say that you were hungry. We can get you some food and in the meantime, you can tell me what happened to Erin and Barry.

"Barry blew it," she said. She got into the car and buckled in. Jim started the car and pulled onto the busy street outside the building. The street was filled with cars that weren't going anywhere quickly. "He said all of the wrong things. He told the police that I heard the future murder."

"What?" Jim turned onto a side street where the cars were moving a little. "I haven't known him very long, but is he always like this?"

"He's always been a little less than normal. I don't know what Erin sees in him. She knows how I feel and how I think she could do better, but she loves him for some reason."

The traffic was beginning to move some, and Jim was trying to figure out which way would be best way to go. As he looked at street signs, he saw a man in blue jeans and a black hooded sweatshirt standing on a corner. The hood was up so that his face was hidden. As they drove by, the man looked up with a scowl and watched the car go by through dark glasses. Jim felt uncomfortable but let it go.

The traffic started to move again, and Jim began to feel better about being back on their way.

Jessi was quiet.

"What are you thinking?" Jim asked.

Jessi didn't look at Jim, but a small smile formed. "Well, I was thinking about back in the lobby of the TV station."

Jim smiled. "And what exactly were you thinking about it?"

"I was just wondering…" As she was talking, she heard sirens growing louder in the distance. She stopped talking and asked Jim, "Aren't you going to pull over?" Just after she asked the question, the sound of the sirens passed by and faded away.

"Why?" Jim asked. "What did you have in mind?"

"Never mind," Jessi said. "There will be emergency vehicles passing by this spot tomorrow." Jessi shook her head. These things happen at the worst times.

"That must be so weird," Jim said. "Actually, I imagine that it's pretty hard to live with. You don't have any idea when it's going to happen, do you?"

"No," she answered, "but it's no more strange than what you hear."

"How's that?"

"Think about it. You don't know what you'll hear at any given time. A siren could come out of nowhere, a woman could scream, and car breaks could squeal. Anything could happen. So whether it's a sound from today or tomorrow, it happens without notice."

Jim nodded. "But you have some notice in that you hear the future sounds. You could come back tomorrow and see the emergency vehicle speed by. Isn't it something that you appreciate sometimes?"

"I wish I didn't have it," she said. "I wish I had never been in that accident and could just live a normal life. I get so tired of not knowing what's real and what's phantom. I get tired of people looking at me like I'm crazy. Just like a moment ago, you wondered why I asked if you would pull over. The sirens sounded real to me, but you heard nothing. I wish I couldn't hear the future."

"You say that, but today, you might save a life because of your abilities. Wouldn't that make it worth the struggle?"

"Might is the key word here, Jim," Jessi said. "We've only got four hours to go, and I still don't know what will happen to stop this. I'm tired and hungry and feeling frustrated right now. I can't help but wonder what today would have been like if I was normal. I wonder what I would do today if I couldn't hear future sounds."

Jim was quiet momentarily and then said, "You probably wouldn't be spending the day with me, and I wouldn't have had the chance to get to know you. People, specifically the guys at work, heard that you hear things. If those guys hadn't been there, you would have left before I arrived in the lot, we wouldn't be trying to stop a murder, and you would be far away from wherever I would be today. But the fact is that you can hear those sounds, and here we are today, together, trying to figure it all out. It's a lot to think about, so maybe we could think better on a full stomach. What do you say we go to Taco Taco and get some food? My treat."

"That sounds really good right now," Jessi said. "Mind if I call Erin and have her and Barry join us?"

"I guess if Barry has to be there," Jim said jokingly, rolling his eyes.

Jessi reached over and playfully pushed his shoulder.

"It's fine," Jim said. "The more the merrier. But, I'm only paying for you and me…and maybe Erin."

Jessi shook her head, laughed a little, and called Erin and let her know. Erin didn't sound happy, and it was hushed over the phone, which meant to Jessi that Barry was probably sulking. Jessi knew Erin better than anyone else and could say one or two things that lightened her mood.

"So Jim's sister-in-law was amazing. Not only did she believe me, but she showed me information about another girl who could do the same thing as me. That was some time ago, but the main thing is that she believed us, and she's working to see what she can do to help. It was excellent news."

"I'm glad someone has some good news since ours was so horrible!" Erin said.

Jessi knew Erin was still mad at Barry and that lunch wouldn't be enjoyable if this mood continued. "It's all working out for the best," Jessi said, "and you never know what events might spin off from your visit to the police. It might have been meant to go that way. Come on, I want to hear a smile in your voice."

It was quiet momentarily, but then Erin said, "I don't wanna."

"Erin?" Jessi said teasing.

Erin sighed. "Okay, fine. You always have to be a little ray of sunshine, right? As always, though, you're right. I guess I just need to wait and see what the future brings. No sense in…"

Jessi heard the screeching of tires through the phone.

"Erin? Is everything okay? What's going on?"

Jim looked concerned, but Jessi held up one finger, indicating that he should wait a moment.

"Stupid jerk!"

Jessi heard the yell from Erin, but not into the phone. She could hear more conversation between Erin and Barry, but much of it was muffled.

When Erin got back on the phone, she asked, "Jessi? Are you still there?"

"Yeah. What's going on? What just happened?"

"Some jerk just pulled out from a side street in front of us and slammed on his brakes! He just sat in front of our car and stared at us. Some weirdo in a black hooded sweatshirt. He glared at us and then sped away."

"Are you guys okay?"

"Yeah. We're fine. Just a little shaken up," Erin said but sounded slightly shaken.

"Let's meet up. I don't know where you guys are now, but could we all get together at Taco Taco for lunch? It would be good for us all to meet and brainstorm again. Jim said it was his treat."

"Yeah, that might be a good idea. I'll let Barry know, and we'll see you there in about twenty minutes. Love you, girl."

"Love you, Erin. See you soon."

"All set," Jessi said to Jim.

"So don't keep me in suspense. What was going on?"

Jessi laughed. "Sorry. I forgot that you couldn't hear the conversation. Some creep in a black, hooded sweatshirt cut them off and glared at them before taking off again. I think that it really scared Erin."

"A black, hooded sweatshirt?" Jim asked. "That's so strange. There was a guy like that a few miles back when we were stuck in traffic. He was standing on the corner, and he just watched us as we drove by."

Jessi hunched her shoulders and raised her hands beside her face, wriggling her fingers at Jim. "Ooo. Creepy! The guy in the black hoodie is everywhere. Look! He's over there, and look, there he is again!" Jessi was having fun pointing out every person on the street with a black hoodie. She looked over at Jim, who was watching her and had stopped smiling.

She saw him looking at the rearview mirror over and over. She turned to look behind them and then back at Jim. "Why do you keep looking in the mirror like that?"

"A car has been behind us for a few minutes now. It seems to take the same turns no matter where we go. We're being followed, but it's probably my imagination."

"Is the driver wearing a black hoodie?" Jessi asked jokingly.

Jim looked up again and said, "As a matter of fact, he is."

Jessi turned and looked. "Could be that whoever is driving is hungry and heading to Taco Taco like we are," she commented and turned back around. "Why would anyone want to follow us?"

"True." Jim switched to a British accent. "But in this world of espionage and undercover work, where murders and mysteries are commonplace, it's not unusual for the spy team of Jim and Jessi to be followed on any particular day, especially when they are on their way to spy central, also known to common folks as, Taco Taco."

They both laughed. At that point, Jessi felt another slight tug at her heart. Her smile and her look lingered. "I like spending time with you, Jim" she said.

"I'm glad," he replied. "Even though it's not a typical first date, I've also enjoyed spending time with you."

"I thought last night was our first date?" Jessi said.

"You said it wasn't a date," Jim replied.

"I didn't say today was a date either," she teased, "but, I guess we could consider it that. Longest first date on record."

They laughed again, and Jim had to admit that this was turning out to be much better than he had hoped.

He saw the restaurant ahead, turned, and pulled into the parking lot. Jim watched in his rearview mirror as the mysterious car passed the lot and drove away. "Guess I was just imagining things about the car. It's gone now," he said. "Not as hungry as we are."

Before they walked to the restaurant, Jessi looked around for Barry's car but didn't see it anywhere. "Do you see Barry's car?" she asked Jim. "It's a little red Toyota."

Jim looked around, but for some reason, there was no red car to be seen. "Nope. Not a single red car anywhere. Perhaps he had it re-painted so that he could better go incognito."

"I seriously doubt that Barry would do that for two reasons; first, he's too cheap to paint his car, and second, he wants to always be the center of attention. Maybe they were just a little farther away than they thought," she said and shrugged, "or maybe they just hit traffic."

However, when she and Jim walked in, they saw Erin sitting alone at one of the tables. They walked over and sat down with her.

"Hi, Erin," Jessi said, sliding beside her. "Boyfriend in the bathroom or just hiding so he can jump out and surprise us?"

Erin looked up at her. She didn't look happy and said with a lack of enthusiasm, "Hi and none of the above."

"Okay, so then where is Barry? He's always hungry, so I thought he'd jump at the chance to eat! Especially if he didn't have to pay for it."

"We got into this huge fight, and he dropped me off. Then he just took off. I have no idea where he went. I want to call him, but I'm now upset with him. In fact, at this point in time, I'm not sure that I ever want to talk to him again. I've really just had it with him. This might be the break-up moment for me, Jess. He hasn't done anything right today, and we've just fought continuously."

"I'm sorry," Jessi said. "He can sometimes be the worst boyfriend ever, but there are times when he's sweet, kind, and loving to you. He might even have a few other good qualities I don't know about. We can talk about it, and then you can weigh the important parts and decide. In the meantime, and I don't mean to be insensitive, do you want anything to eat, or are you too upset?"

Erin shrugged. "You're not being insensitive. We were supposed to meet here to grab a bite to eat, but my stomach is in knots right now, so maybe it's just something to drink. Then you can tell me more about what you learned during your visit with the Channel 7 lady."

"Okay, hun. We'll be right back." Jessi and Jim went to the counter and ordered food. They waited until it was ready, gathering napkins and straws, and then brought everything back to the table.

"Here's your drink." Jessi set the cup down in front of Erin.

She took a large drink. "I guess I was pretty thirsty. Maybe after I'm rehydrated, I'll feel better. Tell me more about what you guys found out."

"So, we went to see Jim's sister-in-law on Channel 7. She seemed really helpful. I think she was a little doubtful at first, even though she had seen someone who had my ability before. She asked for some proof that I can hear sounds and after feeling a little lost I gave her the best demonstration. I wish that you could have been there to see it. I'll tell you all about *that* later. Anyway, she's supposed to call us soon and tell us what she can do to help," Jessi said in between bites.

"That's good news," Erin said, sipping her drink. "I'm so disappointed in Barry. He just wimped out on me. I don't know what's eating him today, but he's certainly not himself. In fact, he hasn't been himself for several days. I just don't know what to do."

Jim said, "Different people react to pressure in different ways. Sometimes, they even react differently depending on the type of pressure. Don't be too hard on him. I'm sure that in some sort of odd way, he felt that he was doing what was best."

"Yeah, but Barry is usually pretty stable. I mean, there are times when he's down about stuff and other times when he seems distraught because he doesn't know what to do. But today, he just seemed like he'd lost it. It's almost like he was a completely different person. And he was so weird around the police today. He was really nervous and not at all like he normally is. This morning, he acted like he just wanted to ignore the day, and then we had this big blow-up, and he took off. I don't know what's going on with him."

"And you don't know where he went?" Jessi asked, taking a sip of her drink.

"No. I think he just wanted to drive around and cool off a bit. It bothers me that he was so incredibly uncomfortable around the police today. It makes me suspicious that something else is going on."

Jim was about to take another bite of his taco when his phone rang.

He looked at the screen and said to Jessi, "It's Lyn." He put his taco down and answered his phone. "Hello."

"Hi, Jimmy! It's Lyn."

"Hey, Lyn. You have some news for us, I take it?"

"Jimmy, I've been doing a lot of thinking about this, trying to figure out a way to intervene unobtrusively but still stop the murder from taking place, and I came up with this idea. I will get a hold of the warehouse owner and have him meet me along with a camera crew at the warehouse at three-thirty. I will tell him we're doing a story on property sales in the county and see if he'll agree to an interview, telling him it might help with the sale. If he says he can't make it, we'll set everything up to do a mock story anyway. That might discourage the killer from showing up or even trap him inside if he's already there. We'll watch for any cars or people approaching and get them on camera. Win, win for us that way."

"That's a great idea, Lyn! What should we do?"

"Just what I told you earlier," Lyn scolded. "Stay away from the warehouse. I don't want you putting yourself in the line of danger. Jimmy, I've seen many of these situations go bad too fast. Even professionals have been hurt and even killed when things don't go according to plan, and there are times when our plan doesn't fit into what the criminal had in mind."

"But Lyn," Jim pleaded, "don't you think we should be there to…"

"No, I don't think you should be anywhere near there! Now, don't make me tell you again."

"But we've been so involved in this that…"

"Jimmy. Shut up and finish eating. I'll give you full credit if there's a capture because of this."

"Okay. I understand. I disagree, but I understand. One last question: how did you know I was eating?"

Lyn laughed, "A good reporter is like a good detective. We gather clues. I could hear the music in the background, trays being emptied into trash bins and other conversations. You're a young man who likes to eat. Ergo, you are at a restaurant."

"You're good, Lyn," Jim laughed. "I'll let everyone here know what's going on. And thank you, Lyn." He ended the call.

Jessi was eager to hear what was going to happen. "Well? What did she say? Don't leave me hanging. How are we going to stop this?"

"She's going to get a hold of the owner and meet him there around 3:30 for an interview. She's thinking that might discourage the killer."

"Cool! Great idea." But Jessi didn't believe her own words. She felt that there was something wrong with the idea. She couldn't put her finger on it. As Jessi was thinking, Erin's phone rang. Jessi figured that it had to be Barry calling to apologize.

Jim was still talking, and Jessi realized that lost in her own feelings, she had stopped listening. "I'm sorry, Jim. My mind wandered. What did you say?"

"The bad news is that she doesn't want us to go to the warehouse."

"What! Still! Doesn't she understand that I need to be there? I heard the scream. I feel connected somehow. I have to be there to make sure it turns out okay."

"I know," Jim said, "but she seems to be very adamant about us not going, and after she explained it to me, I understood why. It's a safety thing. I wouldn't want you or me to get hurt."

"I don't believe this," Jessi said.

"Don't believe what?" Erin asked, putting down her phone. "What did I miss?"

"Jim's sister-in-law is calling the owner to get him out to the warehouse, but we're not supposed to go out there."

"Too late for that," Erin said. "That was Barry. I guess he's back to his old normal self. He actually came up with a good idea. He's coming to pick me up, and we're driving out there to sit and watch. Then, if we see anything suspicious, we can call the cops and get them out there. We're not going to interfere with anything. We're just going to watch from a distance."

120

"Duh," Jessi said, smacking her forehead. "That's brilliant! Why didn't we just do that, to begin with? The killer won't do anything if there's an audience."

"Brilliant, and yet maybe not so smart," Jim said.

"Don't worry," Erin said. "I'll talk to Barry when he gets here. He's going to meet me outside. You guys finish your meals, and I'll call you shortly. We can hook up someplace later. We still have three hours."

The driver in the car across the street watched the restaurant in the sideview mirror, waiting for someone in particular to leave.

# CHAPTER 19

## EMERGENCY

Erin stood up.

Jessi said, "Okay. I'll talk to you in a bit. Call me if you need to or need us to pick you up. You know if Barry changes back to Doctor Jekyll again." Jessi stood, hugged Erin, and watched as she walked out the door.

Jessi sat back down and looked over at Jim. He was staring out the window, lost somewhere beyond the restaurant. She nudged him and brought his mind back inside.

"What? Oh yeah, thanks for joining us, Erin. See you soon." His eyes went back toward the outside.

Jessi laughed and shook her head. "Erin already left you goof." She looked out the window and strained to see what was holding Jim's attention. "What are you looking at?" she asked him, trying again to see what he was looking at. Outside was just the regular beat of the day and the traffic rushing.

"Remember that car that was following us?" he asked.

"Yeah," she responded and continued to look.

Jim brought his hand up slightly and pointed. "It's right over there, sitting across the street, parked at the curb. You see it?"

Jessi nodded. She stared at the car, trying to determine who was in the driver's seat. But all she could see was a shadowy figure who looked like he was talking on a cell phone. She couldn't make out any facial details, and she couldn't see the license plate. She looked as hard as she could and then suddenly jumped when she heard heavy breathing and was tapped on the shoulder. She turned to see Erin, out of breath.

"What are you doing back here? Where's Barry? Did he leave you here again?"

"He just pulled up on the other side of the restaurant," she said quickly. "I'm cutting through to meet him. Act natural."

"Act natural?" Jessi called out to her as Erin ran out the other door, leaving Jim and Jessi to look at each other, perplexed at what had just happened.

Jim turned his attention back to the street, and Jessi followed suit. She looked hard once again at the car. "I think you're imagining things," she said to Jim. "Are you sure that's the same car?"

"Yeah. It is the same car. Why would he be sitting out there? Do you think he's watching us?"

Suddenly, a man ran up to the table, out of breath. He put his hands down heavily on the table, startling Jessi and Jim. They turned to look at the middle-aged man, breathing hard.

"Excuse me. I'm sorry to startle you," he said, huffing and puffing.

"Can we help you?" Jim asked. "Are you okay?"

"I'm Detective O'Malley with the Blue Mountain police department," he wheezed, taking out his badge and showing the couple. "Do you mind if I ask you a few questions?"

Jim looked at Jessi, who shrugged. "I guess not," he replied. "Did I park in a bad spot or something? What's this about?"

O'Malley replaced his badge and was finally catching his breath. "No. Your car, as far as I know, is fine. Do you mind if I sit down? I'm not used to running this much."

"Um, sure," Jim said. He moved toward the window and allowed O'Malley to slide into the small booth.

"I'm sure you're wondering what's going on. Oh wait, you did ask me that, didn't you? Do you have any ID on you? I'm sorry, but I must be certain I know with whom I'm speaking."

"Uh yeah, sure. It's here in my pants pocket. Give me a second."

The tight quarters of the table and booth made it difficult for Jim to grab his wallet, and when he did finally drag it from his pocket, change and his keys came out, spilling to the floor.

"I'll get it," Jessi said, and she got under the table to pick up the keys and loose change. She grabbed her purse and put it all inside except for the wallet, which she handed to Jim.

"Thanks, Jess," Jim said. He removed his license from his wallet and handed it to O'Malley, who looked it over. He took out a notepad, wrote down some information from the license, and then handed it back.

"Thank you, James, or do you go by Jim?" O'Malley asked.

"Yeah, I go by Jim," Jim replied.

O'Malley asked Jessi, "Do you have some ID on you, ma'am?"

"What is this about? Why do you need to see my ID? You briefly flashed your badge, but anyone can get a badge from eBay or even the dollar store. Before I give you such personal information, I'm sure you'll understand if I ask to see more than just a badge from you, sir."

O'Malley raised his eyebrows. "I don't mind at all. In fact, I wish that more people would ask that very thing." O'Malley stood from the table and reached back into his jacket pocket, pulling out his faux leather badge holder. He opened it up and handed it to Jessi. She saw the badge on one side and his identification card on the other.

Satisfied with the identification, she handed it back to O'Malley. "Thanks," she said with a smile and folded her hands on the tabletop.

O'Malley sat back down and looked expectantly at Jessi across the table.

"May I see your ID now, miss?" O'Malley said.

"I'm sorry. Why did you need to see that again?"

O'Malley sighed. "I just like to know who I'm talking to. Is there a reason you don't want me to see your ID? Have you committed a crime? Are you wanted in seven states for something? I could always ask you to come with me, and we could talk down at the station if you'd like. I'm trying to be nice."

Jessi realized that she was being difficult and that it was her defensive attitude due to her secret. "No, I haven't committed a crime, and now I'm not wanted in any states. I apologize. It's been a rough day, and I feel a little ornery. I'll get my license out for you. Just a sec." She reached into her purse, brought out her license, and showed O'Malley. After he wrote down her information, he said, "Thank you, Jessica."

"Jessi," she grumbled, putting her information back in her purse.

"Sorry, Jessi, and thank you for letting me know. You'd be surprised how many people just let you talk to them using a formal name, and they don't tell you what they normally go by."

"So Detective, um. O'Malley was it?" Jim said.

O'Malley nodded.

"I know you didn't just randomly pick us to talk to, and I'm pretty sure you didn't decide to just join us for lunch to discuss the weather. So how can we help you?"

"Yes, well, I'm sorry to disturb your lunch, but I have a matter of great importance. I imagine you're both busy and have plans for the day, so I'll get to the point. The woman leaving here stopped by your table before exiting the other door. I believe her name is Erin. How well do you know her?"

Jim and Jessi exchanged quick glances, then Jessi said, "She's a pretty good friend of mine. We've known each other for years. Why do you ask? Is she in trouble?"

"She's not in any trouble," O'Malley said. "She and her husband stopped by the police station today. They came into my office to visit and mentioned something about a murder that would be happening today. I'm just trying to follow up on their concerns. You two wouldn't happen to know anything about that, would you?"

"Wait a minute," Jim said, smiling. "A murder? Although that sounds very intriguing, it sounds like something from a television show. Are we on some show like COPS or something? Where's the camera?" Jim started looking around, smiling and waving.

O'Malley sighed. "You know, Jim, I've had a very trying day, and I'd like to get some answers sometime before I die. This is a serious thing, and I don't need or appreciate any smart-aleck remarks." O'Malley's smile had disappeared, and he looked like a stern father about to ground his children.

"She's not married," Jessi said.

O'Malley was taken aback at the statement. "What?"

"You said she came in with her husband. They aren't married. I just wanted to make sure you had the facts straight. I know that's important," Jessi said.

O'Malley ran his fingers through his hair. He looked at Jessi. His face reflected the strain he was feeling, and his look made Jessi just a little uncomfortable. "Okay. Now that we have their personal relationship established, can we please get back to the topic I came to discuss? The murder."

"So they said there was going to be a murder. Did they say how they knew this was going to happen?" Jessi asked, but she already knew the answer and suddenly felt regret even bringing it up.

O'Malley fixed his gaze on Jessi and locked eyes with her. "They said they had a friend who heard the murder before it happened. You wouldn't happen to know who that would be, would you?" O'Malley knew from the look on Jessi's face and years of interrogating people that she knew the answer.

Jessi's level of discomfort was growing. She felt trapped. She wanted to tell this man the truth but feared what might happen afterward. She needed time to think.

"You say that someone heard the murder before it happened?" Jim said, "How does that work? I'm not sure that something like that is a common event."

"Oh my goodness," Jessi said suddenly. "I'm so sorry. These huge drinks are too much for me. I've really got to use the bathroom. Can you guys excuse me for just one moment? I really need to go." She looked panicked and started scooting out of the booth before she had an answer.

O'Malley sighed again. He needed answers that didn't seem to be coming. He wondered if he was wasting time, but this was his best lead. He had to keep at it and find out what was going on. These two knew something. Now, he had to find out what it was. "Go ahead. But please hurry. If what they said has any merit to it, the murder is going to happen soon. I don't want that, and I hope you don't either. Something needs to be done and needs to be done now."

"I agree," Jessi said, "and I promise to hurry."

Jessi slid entirely out of the booth and hurried off toward the bathrooms, leaving poor Jim alone with the Detective next to him in the booth.

Jim managed a weak smile and looked out the window to see if the mysterious car was still there. To his surprise, the car was gone. He looked up and down the street as far as he could, but there was no sign.

"What are you looking for?" O'Malley asked.

"Huh? Oh, nothing really. Just a car that I was concerned about."

"Why were you concerned about a car? What's going on?"

"When we went to the restaurant, I thought a car was following us. Then I noticed it was parked across the street, with the driver just sitting in it and looking at the restaurant, and now it's gone. It wasn't you, was it?"

"No," O'Malley said. "It wasn't me. Where was it parked?"

Jim turned to look out the window again to show him where the mystery car had been. As he looked, he saw his car speeding out of the parking lot with Jessi behind the wheel. "Shoot!" Jim yelled. "She took my car! I need to stop her!" Jim started to push his way out of the booth but was blocked by an angry O'Malley.

"Hold on a minute. Who took your car?" O'Malley asked, starting to get a sick feeling in his stomach.

"Jessi! She's leaving in my car." Jim suddenly felt a sinking feeling in his stomach. He thought he knew where she was going, and now he had no way to stop her. He couldn't think. He was beginning to feel panicked. He wanted to push O'Malley out of the seat and run after her, but he knew it wouldn't do any good. His mind raced, but his thoughts were interrupted by O'Malley's voice.

"Jim," he said very seriously, "you need to focus. You need to tell me what's going on, and you need to do it now. I need answers so that I can stop this thing. An innocent life is at stake; you and I are the only two people who can stop it right now. And since I believe you know more than what you've told me so far, which has been nothing, if this woman dies, you can be charged with obstructing justice and interfering with a police investigation. I could probably get away with charging you with accessory to murder. I'm sure you don't want any of those on your record. So start talking and tell me everything so that we can stop this. You want that, don't you, Jim?"

"But my car," Jim started.

"Jim, look at me." Jim looked at O'Malley. "Do you know anything about what will happen involving this murder? You need to tell me if you want to stop it and if you want your car back. I need some answers."

Jim nodded, "Yeah. Okay. Jessi is the girl that can hear future sounds. She's been able to do that for years, and everything she hears comes true. Yesterday, at the warehouse, she heard a girl screaming something about someone trying to kill her, and that's what set this whole thing in motion. We've been trying all day to find someone to help and someone who would believe us. Now, things are falling apart. I'm worried that Jessi's on her way to the warehouse to try and stop this murder from happening. What are we going to do? I don't want her getting hurt." Jim wasn't sure if what he just did was the right thing to do, but at this point, he felt it was the only thing to do. He gave O'Malley a pleading look that convinced him this was no joke.

If this man was crazy, like he thought of Erin and Barry before, then he was just crazy enough to believe his own story.

O'Malley thought about what to do. "My car is out in the lot," O'Malley told Jim. "Let's go. You ride with me and show me where this warehouse is. We can still get there in time, but I swear, if this is a joke, you will not see the light of day again for as long as I can keep you behind bars."

"Thank you!" Jim said and almost pushed O'Malley out of the seat. "It's not a joke. We have to get going and try to beat Jessi to the warehouse."

"Assaulting a police officer is not going to help your case," O'Malley said, trying to lighten up the moment. He exited the booth, and the two men hurried to the door.

They stepped out and took a few steps into the parking lot when Jim stopped. "What time is it?" he asked O'Malley.

O'Malley looked at his watch. Jim thought it strange that this man wore a watch. Not many people wore them anymore. "It's three o'clock," he said.

"We only have fifty minutes," Jim said. Jessi said that, according to when she heard the sound, the murder would take place at three fifty. The things she hears always happen precisely twenty-four hours after she hears them." Jim looked around and remembered that his car was gone. O'Malley started to walk off, and Jim followed. O'Malley unlocked the car and motioned for Jim to get in.

"So, where is the warehouse again?" O'Malley asked.

"It's off of Crossroads Boulevard. It's not hard to find and should only take about twenty minutes to get there."

They sped down the road, and O'Malley radioed for a few officers to meet him at the warehouse.

"So tell me more about this thing that Jessica claims she can do?" O'Malley said to Jim. "Quite honestly, this all sounds like a crazy story you could only find in a fantasy novel or something. I hope you understand if I'm still skeptical about this."

"I understand. It's Jessi. She was in an accident when she was a teenager, about six years or so ago. She died in the accident but was revived in the ambulance. After the accident, she could hear the sounds of future events."

"She was in an accident and died?" O'Malley said. "Does she remember anything other than what people have told her?"

"I don't think so," Jim said. "Honestly, she and I have discussed what she can do regarding hearing the future, but we haven't discussed the actual event. She told me about the accident and her doctor afterward, but nothing in between. Why?"

"My wife was killed in an accident, also about six years ago. She wasn't as lucky as Jessi. A drunk driver drifted across the centerline and into my wife's lane. They couldn't do anything to save her, but because of that, I remember looking at many records of automobile accidents back then, but I don't remember anything about Jessi's."

"I'm so sorry to hear about your wife. That must have been hard."

"It was pretty hard at first, and honestly, there's not a day that goes by where I don't miss her, but I ended up immersing myself in my work. It made me so good at police work that I was promoted to Detective. I consider what happened to my wife to be murder, so I like to be involved in solving to all murders in our area when I can." O'Malley was quiet in thought. "So, as I said, I poured over so many car accidents and paid special attention to anywhere a person died."

It was a bus," Jim said. "She was on the bus taking her and her friends to a martial arts demonstration when the bus swerved and rolled."

O'Malley felt himself grow pale. "O'Donnell," he said softly. "I do remember now. And I seem to remember something else. I knew her father socially back then. Not very well, but I did talk to him occasionally. That was just before I dropped out of the social scene. I couldn't stand to go out without my wife. But anyway, I knew her father and remember him being distraught one night. I took him aside and asked what was wrong and if there was anything I could do. He mentioned something about his daughter and how worried he was about her. Of course, being a police officer, I assumed that she was into drugs or running around with a bad group of kids, so I offered to help. He simply said that it had something to do with her hearing an accident and that he figured it would be okay with time. He said he didn't want to burden me with the details since he knew about my wife. I recall he left after that, and I didn't see him again. Funny how you remember things. I always wondered what he meant by that. Now I think I know."

"Small world, eh?" Jim said. "I've got to tell you, when I first learned about Jessi's ability, I didn't know what to think. I had heard rumors at work, but when she told me, it was right after hearing this murder. You would have been convinced if you could have seen the fear in her eyes and heard the panic in her voice. It was as if she had just really heard a murder. She was pretty shaken up. So, either she was putting a pretty good act, or she really heard it. As much as I've come to know Jessi, I believe she really hears what she hears. The sounds of tomorrow, as well as the sounds of today, so to speak. I feel bad for her and can see how much it weighs on her."

Jim and O'Malley were quiet momentarily when Jim's cell phone rang.

"Hello?" he said, "Hey Lyn, what's up?"

"Jimmy, I spoke with the owner of the warehouse. I investigated him and came up with some interesting facts…" Lyn continued speaking with Jim about what she had discovered.

"What?" he said. "You're kidding! Have you told the police?"

O'Malley looked over at Jim. "Told the police what? Whom are you talking to?"

"Hang on, Lyn," he said into the phone, then to O'Malley, "I'm talking to my sister-in-law, and I'll tell you in a minute. Just keep driving and drive faster!" Jim turned his attention back to the phone. "Lyn? Are you still there? Sorry to put you off, but I'm in a cop car." Jim listened as his sister spoke. "Yes, with a cop," he said sarcastically.

O'Malley continued to glance over at Jim on the phone. He watched Jim's actions and reactions to things that were being said. He was curious and wanted to know what this conversation was about. He would need to wait, however, while Lyn continued to explain what she had discovered during her investigation.

"That name sounds really familiar," he said to Lyn, "What all did you find out about him?" There was a pause, and then Jim blurted out, "Wait! I do know him! But it was from a very long time ago. You wouldn't happen to know what kind of car he drives, would you?" Another pause. "That's what I was afraid of. I think he was following us today. Lyn, Jessi took my car. I think she's headed out there. Is there any way that you can meet me there?" Jim looked over at O'Malley, then slipped back into the phone conversation. "Great! See you in a few."

Jim momentarily stared into space out of the passenger's window and then turned to O'Malley. "Can you turn on lights and siren and go faster?"

"Kid, this isn't a cruiser. It's a plain car. I have some features that would make you jump if you were in front of me, but I have to be totally and one hundred percent convinced that this is an emergency before I radio in that I'm running hot to…"

"There's going to be a murder in," he looked at his phone, "in twenty-five minutes. Isn't that reason enough? We've got to get moving."

O'Malley had been looking at Jim while he was talking. Jim glanced up and instinctively grabbed the dashboard in panic. "Look out!" Jim shouted.

O'Malley turned and slammed on the brakes. His car quickly screeched to a stop only inches away from the stopped car in front of him. He glanced up into the rearview mirror and saw the car behind him do the same, just stopping inches from his car. Nothing moved. Cars quietly idled in the roadway. Jim rolled down the window and looked up ahead. Cars were backed up for about a quarter of a mile, and a big accident blocked the way. It must have just happened. There were not even any emergency vehicles on the scene yet.

O'Malley turned up the radio and heard the chatter as emergency vehicles were called to respond to the accident.

"Can we turn around?" Jim pleaded.

O'Malley rolled down his window and looked back. The cars were lining up behind him. The oncoming lane was clear, but he was too close to the car in front of him. He put the car in reverse and could see on the backup camera that the car behind him was also too close. "I don't know how we can turn around," he said. "Not enough room to move either forward or backward."

Jim heard more chatter on the radio regarding the accident. He thought about Jessi. *We've come too far to let this murder happen*, he thought to himself. He turned to O'Malley. "I'm not a cop," he said, "But I have an idea. Let me know if this will work."

# CHAPTER 20

## MURDER

Jessi pulled into the warehouse parking lot in Jim's car. Once she had parked, she turned off the engine and listened to the surrounding noises of nature, looking around. There were no other cars in the parking lot, and the warehouse looked as it had the day before, except that the entrance door was closed. She remembered the door being open when she left the day before. She couldn't hear anything. Nature was quiet for now, and nothing moved.

She wondered where Lyn and her camera crew were. They should have been here. They might be running behind. She looked around again until she was convinced that it was safe to get out of the car. She opened the door slowly and stepped out cautiously. Maybe she wasn't as convinced as she thought. She was painfully aware of the crunching of the gravel under her feet. Every sound seemed to be magnified. She could hear the sound of the wind rustling leaves and even cars traveling on the nearby highway. She closed the door as quietly as she could. She stood and looked around again. Everything looked normal. A crow landed in the lot behind her and let out a loud "CAW." Jessi jumped and turned. She waved her arms, and the bird flew away. The flapping sound seemed to thunder in her ears. *Stupid crow*, she thought. She watched as the crow flew up, then over toward the warehouse. As she watched the crow fly over the building, she thought she saw a movement by the far corner of the structure. She looked and watched. Nothing. No movement. No sound. But there was something. She was sure of it. A shadowy figure, possibly the same one that had been following them all day, or perhaps a shadowy figure from the depths of her mind. She didn't know.

Jessi slowly walked toward the warehouse and could could hear her heart beating hard and fast. She walked quietly until she reached the entrance. The door was slightly ajar, and she put her ear close to the slight opening to see if she could hear something, anything, which might indicate activity inside. She heard nothing except her own breathing. She pushed the door, and it opened slowly, quietly, and effortlessly.

The inside of the warehouse was exactly the way it was the day before. It was mostly dark, with only small shafts of light shining through the overhead row of windows along the upper edge of the building. She took a few steps inside and stood quietly in the darkness, allowing her eyes to adjust to the dim light. She listened. There was a noise. It was slight, but she could hear it. It was the muffled sound of a woman struggling. Jessi walked a little further into the darkness toward the office. The light behind her vanished, and she heard the entrance door close with a slight click of the latch. She turned and looked behind her but saw no one there.

She continued walking toward the small office area ahead of her. She cautiously rounded the corner and saw a door, slightly open, with a dim light shining out into the warehouse through a small crack. Jessi approached the door and looked inside. She could see the partial form of a woman sitting in a chair with her head bent forward. Jessi carefully pushed the door, which creaked as it opened. The terrified woman in the chair looked up. It was Erin! She saw Jessi creeping into the room and immediately started shaking her head back and forth. She tried calling out to Jessi, but the tape on her mouth allowed only muffled sounds to escape.

Jessi crept over to the chair, and half whispered, "Erin! What happened?" She carefully removed the tape from Erin's mouth and then moved around to the back of her chair to untie her hands. "Who did this to you? Where's Barry?"

"Jessi," Erin said, panicking, "you've got to get out of here. He's here for you, not me. It's all about you!"

"Who's here for me?" Jessi asked, still untying Erin's hands. "What are you talking about?"

Jessi heard the door slam shut, and the dim light suddenly went out, like a candle flame snuffed out with the wind from the slamming door. She froze.

"He's here," Erin whispered.

"That's right, Jessi. I'm here." The voice was deep and ominous.

"I'm not afraid of you," Jessi said. "What do you want?"

"You, Jessi," the voice said. "I want you." The light slowly increased back to the slight, dim state that it was earlier.

She looked up to see a man's figure standing in front of the door. The dim light made it difficult to identify who it was at first. Jessi stood, and the man's face became recognizable. "Jake?" Jessi asked, surprised to see her old Kung Fu classmate.

"That's right, Jessi."

Jessi stepped toward Jake, but he turned quickly and hit her head with a spinning roundhouse kick. Jessi flew across the room, and her head hit the wall. She slumped to the ground.

Erin screamed at Jake, "Leave her alone! What's the matter with you?"

Jake whirled around to face Erin. "What's the matter with me? Oh, don't even pretend like you don't know. You were there, Erin. You know."

"I was where?" Erin asked, "And I know what?"

"Erin, Erin, Erin." Jake grabbed her by the hair, bringing his face close to hers. "You were at the Kung Fu school that day. The day of the demonstration when we were supposed to go to the park on the bus. Remember the bus? That day, I stood up in the bus, and the bus was hit? That day when she was supposed to die, when she should have died? That day changed everything for me. After the accident, our instructor was all over me. He told me how careless I was and how something like this should never have happened. I was kicked out of the program and told to never come back. I decided to train myself in the arts and get Jessi to forgive me. I loved her. I've always loved her. But the accident drove her away from me. She never even noticed me after that. She always walked around in a daze. I'd watch her, but she never ever noticed me. I tried to get her to notice me. I worked hard and became successful, but she still didn't notice me. She ruined my life. I bought this warehouse and even tried to start a business to distract myself, but she continually crept into my thoughts, ruining my life. I started to practice how I would get her to leave my thoughts. I killed others who looked like her. I figured out the perfect way to end her life and my life of torture. And now, the day is here. Now I can be free."

Jake was so focused on Erin that he didn't notice Jessi slowly standing up. She was shaky, but she was determined to survive. She crept up behind Jake as he spoke to Erin about the past, ranting and carrying on like the crazy man he had become. When she was within striking distance, Erin told Jake, "Maybe you'll be free, but maybe not the way you think."

Jessi wound up and delivered a back hammer blow to the side of Jake's head. The powerful blow caused him to reel, and he stumbled toward the wall. Jessi ran over to Erin and started to untie her again. Jake, only dazed, pushed himself away from the wall and picked up a nearby plastic chair, throwing it at Jessi. She held up her hands and blocked the oncoming object. Jake followed it across the room, grabbed Jessi's shoulders, and threw her across the room. She fell, and Jake lunged to the floor and grabbed Jessi's ankle. He swiped at her with a knife and cut her ankle superficially. Jessi kicked at Jake's face with her free foot, hitting him in the nose. The sudden pain caused Jake to let go of her ankle, allowing her to get up and stumble toward the office door. As she reached the door and was able to open it, but Jake, determined now to finish the job, got up and grabbed for her. The two of them struggled for control of the knife. Jessi would try using leverage to make him drop the knife, but Jake would counter each move.

As they struggled, Jessi thought she heard a noise in the central part of the warehouse. She screamed, "Help me! He's trying to kill me!"

She realized then that the person she had been so intent on saving this whole day was her. It was her life that was in jeopardy, and she was going to be killed. In her attempt to save a life, she put herself in the position of being the victim.

Jake grabbed Jessi by the hair and pulled her back into his grasp. He brought his right hand around and over her shoulder and held the knife to her throat. Jessi grabbed his arm and froze. The two stood in the office doorway, breathing hard. Jake had the upper hand now, and Jessi's mind raced.

"You ruined my life," Jake hissed in her ear.

"So I heard," Jessi said, "but you know I never meant to hurt you. You know that, right?"

"Never meant to hurt me?" Jake laughed. "Then why did I hurt so much every day that I saw you? I don't think I was hurting myself. It was you who was hurting me. You!"

"You're wrong, Jake. You're so totally wrong. I always thought you were the best martial artist in the school, not just in our class, but in the school. I used to love to watch you work out. I used to wish that I could be half as good as you were. I used to wish that you would teach me what you knew."

"Oh, right!" Jake said, tightening his grip around her shoulders. "You lie! You never even noticed me when I worked out. You didn't even know I was alive!"

"No, no. I always admired you," Jessi said. "I thought that you never liked me. I was so shy back then. I didn't have the nerve to approach you. You were such a good martial artist and so good-looking. I thought you

136

could get any girl you wanted, and why would you want someone as plain as me? You were like a movie star to me. The thought of coming up and talking to you made me feel so shy. Don't you remember? I used to watch you all of the time."

As Jessi spoke, Jake thought. He thought back on the hundreds of practices. Could he see her standing off on the side of the room, watching him practice? Did she turn away when he looked over? Yes, she would.

Jessi could feel that his grip was loosening. She prepared to make a move if his grip loosened just enough.

Jake continued to think about those times. She would turn away. Was it because she was shy? "No!" he said aloud, tightening his grip even more. Jessi gasped for air. "You would watch sometimes, but then you would turn away and laugh. You didn't care for me. You didn't love me the way I loved you. You're just saying these things to try and save your own skin!"

"I am, Jake," Jessi said.

"What?" Jake was confused for a moment.

"I am trying to save my own skin. Wouldn't you? If you were in my position, would you do whatever you needed to do to save your own life?" Jessi switched tactics and hoped.

"That's not really an issue now, is it Jessi? The fact is, my life isn't in jeopardy." Jake growled.

"Are you sure about that?" From the office doorway, Jake looked out into the dimly lit main area of the warehouse. Two figures stood in the dark corner. As Jake strained to see who was there, the two figures stepped forward into the better light. Jessi looked and recognized Jim and O'Malley. Her heart soared, and she prayed that they would help her get out of this mess. O'Malley continued, "It seems to me that Jessi isn't the only one facing a life-and-death issue right now." O'Malley held a gun leveled at Jake.

Jake held Jessi tighter to him, using her as a shield.

"Who are you?" Jake called out.

O'Malley inched forward. "I'm Detective O'Malley with the Blue Mountain Police Department. Did I hear Jessi call you Jake? Jake, you need to let her go."

"I'll kill her if you come any closer," Jake said.

O'Malley stopped moving forward but didn't lower his gun. "I know you will, Jake. That's why I stopped. Now, let's talk about what you want and how we can end this so that no one gets hurt. I think that's what we all want, isn't it? Enough people have died, and no one else has to die today."

"No," Jake yelled. "You're wrong. She was supposed to die six years ago. She's not supposed to be here now. She was never supposed to live through that accident. That's why she was the only one who died. And because they brought her back, my life was cursed. It's her fault."

"Jake," O'Malley said, "It's not her fault that the paramedics revived her. She didn't have any say in that. Have you thought about that, Jake?"

Jessi could see that O'Malley was trying to shift the blame in Jake's mind and confuse him. But she felt him start shaking his head, and she saw O'Malley sneak another step forward.

"Stay back!" Jake yelled again. "I'll kill her! I swear I will."

"I know you will, Jake. Just like you killed those other women. I know you won't hesitate to kill Jessi if we don't come to an agreement. And Jessi knows that you'll kill her too, don't you, Jessi?"

"I do know," Jessi said. "I also know that Jake has turned into a very hard person. He's forgotten all of his martial arts training."

"What do you mean?" Jake said, "I can still beat anyone, and I mean anyone, who would challenge me. I train every day. I haven't forgotten anything!"

"That's not what I meant, Jake," Jessi said. "You are still a good martial artist, a great martial artist! But you've forgotten what the martial arts are all about. You've forgotten what makes them great. You've forgotten the basic foundation of the art."

"Oh?" Jake said sarcastically. "You think I've forgotten the basics? Well, miss know-it-all. Why don't you enlighten me? Why don't you tell this the big secret that I've forgotten? What is this basic thing that I supposedly forgot?"

"Character," Jessi said. "Character. The art is nothing if you don't have good character."

"C'mon, Jake," O'Malley said, inching another small amount forward. "Show some good character and let her go. It's not too late. You can do this, Jake. Set an example for other students. Show them the right things to do."

Again, Jake went back in time in his mind. He could hear the instructor talking about character. He could hear the instructor telling Jake what great character he had. But then his thoughts turned back to the instructor yelling at him for showing off on the bus, saying that it was all his fault, and telling him he could never train there again.

"NO!" Jake yelled. "It's not my fault!" He looked at O'Malley and said,

"Now, here's what's going to happen. You're going to back off and get out of here, or she dies in the next ten seconds."

"Jake, think about what you're doing," O'Malley said.

"I have thought about it!" Jake cried, "And I'm ready to do this. I've already killed more women than I can count, and one more won't matter."

"But you didn't love the others, Jake. You love Jessi. You've always loved her. And now you have her, and you're just going to throw that away? This is your second chance. How many people are granted a second chance, Jake? If you're willing to throw that away, I think there's got to be something more, don't you, Jessi?"

"I guess," Jessi said, slightly confused at what O'Malley was getting at.

"Wouldn't you like to get to the bottom of it all, Jessi?" O'Malley said.

Jessi thought about the words. He emphasized, 'Get to the bottom of it'. What did he mean, and what was he trying to say?

"The bottom of it?" she asked.

"Yes, Jessi. Wouldn't you like to get to the root of what is happening?" O'Malley said.

Jessi suddenly realized what O'Malley was asking her to do. It was a risk, but if she did it correctly, there was a chance that she wouldn't get any more hurt than she already was. She steeled herself against whatever might happen as she raised her right foot and turned it quickly outward. Her left ankle burned as she put her weight on it. The cut must have been deeper than she thought. She took the outside of her raised foot and raked down Jake's shin, ending with a foot-breaking heel stomp on his instep. He immediately released her and raised his hurt foot. When he did, Jessi dropped to the ground, and O'Malley fired his weapon. Jessi saw Jake crumple to the ground. O'Malley ran over to Jake, and Jim ran over to Jessi. O'Malley checked Jake for life and then radioed, "This is O'Malley. I need paramedics at Sixty-five hundred Crossroads Boulevard. Send two units."

Jessi sat up and smiled at Jim. "Thank you for coming to my rescue."

"I guess we're even now," Jim said.

"Nah. I saved you from four guys. You saved me from one. Not quite even yet, she teased him and then collapsed.

He cradled her in his arms and waited for the paramedics to arrive.

"Jessi! Are you okay? What's going on?" Erin called from the office.

O'Malley ran into the small office. Erin's eyes grew wide when she saw

O'Malley. "Thank goodness it's you," she cried. "I heard a gunshot and was afraid that…"

"Jessi's going to be fine," O'Malley said quietly.

Erin started to cry. The relief of knowing that everything would be okay finally hit her. O'Malley walked over and finished untying her. As he loosened the ropes, Erin said, "Please help Barry. He's tied up over in that corner." She nodded to a dark corner of the room. O'Malley looked and could barely see the dark image of Barry lying in a curled-up position. After he freed Erin, O'Malley walked over and untied Barry.

Barry didn't move at first, and O'Malley was afraid that he had been hurt. Then he groaned and moved his head. O'Malley slapped him lightly on the face, and Barry opened his eyes with a "Hey! Knock it off!"

The ambulances arrived. Jake was loaded up and hauled off under police supervision. Jessi was lifted onto a gurney and strapped down. They wheeled her to the ambulance, with Jim walking beside her. He was shaking but glad she was okay.

Jim looked up to see the Channel 7 news trucks arrive. Lyn jumped out of the car and ran over to Jim and Jessi.

"Jim," Lyn said, slightly out of breath, "I'm so sorry we couldn't get here any sooner. Traffic on the main road was terrible. There was a bad accident that we couldn't get around."

"I know," Jim said. "O'Malley and I were stuck in the same mess. In fact, we got there just after it happened."

"How did you manage to get around it?"

"It was a brilliant idea on O'Malley's part, really. We were going to wait until the emergency vehicles showed up and then flag one down and use their car, but when O'Malley realized how long that would take, he devised another plan. He turned on his lights and siren. The poor guy in the little sports car in front of us. I thought he was going to have a heart attack! Anyway, there some construction guys in several trucks were also stuck in the line. They got out and came to see if they could help, and then they moved the little sports car sideways! They actually picked it up, with the driver still in it, and moved it out of the way so that we could get through and go around the accident. It was pretty amazing. I've decided that someday, I want a siren in my car."

"Ain't gonna happen, buddy," O'Malley said.

Jim laughed. "I'm just messin' with you."

Jim turned his attention back toward Jessi. "Are you okay?"

"You followed me!" she said to him.

"Yeah, well, you stole my car," he chided. "Besides, what you did was just stupid, and I couldn't let you be stupid by yourself."

"Yeah," Jessi said, "I'm tired of being stupid alone."

The paramedics gathered on both ends of the gurney and started to move it toward the ambulance.

"I'll see you at the hospital," Jim said to Jessi, then leaned over and kissed her.

"Taking advantage of a girl when she's down?" Jessi asked.

"I just didn't want you to kick my butt if I tried that when you were standing. But you're tied down, so I didn't have to worry about it."

"I guess I'll just have to kick your butt later," Jessi said and smiled.

"I didn't think about that," Jim replied.

The paramedics loaded Jessi into the ambulance, shut the doors, and drove off to the hospital. Jim stood silently but happy as he watched them drive away. O'Malley walked up to Jim and put his hand on his shoulder.

"Well, Jim," he said. "I'm going to have to arrest you now."

Jim turned suddenly and looked at O'Malley with a perplexed look. "What?"

"Yeah, let's go," he said.

"For what?" Jim was starting to panic.

"Well, let's see," O'Malley started, "Lying to an officer of the law, obstruction of justice, illegal parking…" O'Malley reached for his handcuffs, then looked at Jim and winked. "Just messin' with you," he said and laughed.

Jim was relieved and sighed. "You're kind of weird for a cop."

"And you're just kind of weird," O'Malley replied. "But I like you."

"I'm going to go meet Jessi at the hospital and make sure she's okay," Jim said and started to walk off.

"So you got your keys back from Jessi?" O'Malley asked, stopping Jim in his tracks.

"Shoot! I forgot all about her having the keys," Jim said.

"That's why I'm the cop. I pay attention to details. So, sunshine, what are you going to do now? Steal my car?"

"I don't have the keys to that one either," Jim said. "You wouldn't happen to be going to the hospital, would you? If so, could I catch a ride with you?"

"Actually," O'Malley said, "I need to get a statement from your girlfriend, so yeah, I'm heading over there. But you'll have to take a taxi back. And don't make me impound your car for being parked on private property."

Jim was smiling. "I like that."

"What, having your car impounded?"

"No," Jim said, still smiling. "I like the sound of Jessi being my girlfriend."

O'Malley shook his head. "C'mon. Let's go."

Erin and Barry were being wheeled out on gurneys to another waiting ambulance. Erin's gurney arrived just before Jim left.

Erin said, "Are you coming to the hospital, Jim?"

"As long as the good detective here doesn't leave without me!"

O'Malley smiled. "It's tempting. It really is."

"One more second?" Jim asked.

O'Malley sighed. "One more, but I have to get going soon. I'm on overtime!"

Jim approached Barry and asked, "Are you doing okay?"

"Yeah," Barry replied. "But I feel like I've been run over by a truck."

Jim laughed. "So what happened to your car?"

"That's a really long story, and I think Jessi deserves to hear it too. Let's get to the hospital and see how everyone is doing, and I'll tell you all about it there."

"Deal!" Jim said.

Lyn looked at Jim, "If you don't mind, I'm coming to the hospital as well. This is going to make a great story. Although, for the sake of believability, I may have to twist it just a little. See you there, Jimmy."

The paramedics loaded Erin and Barry into the ambulance and drove off. Jim turned in time to see O'Malley walking off toward his car and hurried to catch up.

# CHAPTER 21

## EXPLANATIONS

Jessi sat in the emergency room waiting for the doctor to come back with the results of the exams and the tests. Jessi thought that he looked familiar when she first saw him. When he finally walked back in, she realized that he was the same doctor who treated her after the bus accident six years earlier. He smiled at her and walked over, holding a tablet. He entered in a few keystrokes and brought up the results of the CAT scan.

"Well, Jessi," the doctor smiled, "I believe things could have been much worse for you. Looks like you suffered a mild concussion, a bump on the head, a small and superficial cut on your throat, and, of course, that cut on your ankle. I think the ankle laceration was the worst of it, and fortunately, no tendons were involved. You might have a small scar there, but that will be it. Go home, rest for a few days, and you should be fine."

Jessi shook her head. "This is really déjà vu!"

The doctor ran his finger over the screen of his tablet and pulled up Jessi's records. "This is similar to what happened to you several years ago," the doctor said. "Head trauma. Cuts and bruises. The only difference is that last time you died in the ambulance, and this time, you only came close to dying."

"When you phrase it that way, it's not very comforting," Jessi said.

"I don't exactly remember the circumstances surrounding your last visit," the doctor said, thinking out loud, "Oh wait! Wasn't it a bus crash and something to do with your martial arts class?"

"Yeah," Jessi said. "That's the only part of that day I remember, being here in the hospital."

"I seem to recall something else, too. Let me check another file real quick here." The doctor swiped across the face of his tablet several times and then showed Jessi two images. One was the CT scan from several years ago, and the other was today. He looked at both, and his face showed signs of concern.

"What's wrong, doctor?"

"Well, I'm looking at the scans we did from your last accident and the ones we did today. There is a difference between them." He pointed to the old scan. "In this one, the blood flow is mostly in this part of your brain," he said, pointing to the photo, "showing increased activity there, but it's the one we did today that has changed. It's more normal-ish. I guess that's a good sign. Do you feel any different?"

"Not really. I actually feel perfect! Thanks for that information, doctor."

Erin, Barry, and Jim stood outside the small, curtained area where Jessi was being examined. Erin said, 'Knock, knock. Are you decent? Can we come in and see you?"

Jessi looked at the doctor, who nodded his approval.

"Yeah. Come on in," she answered.

The three entered, asking Jessi different questions simultaneously. Jessi held up her hands. "Whoa, whoa, whoa, guys. Not all at once. How about just one at a time?"

"I'll let you and your friends talk," the doctor said. "A nurse will be in soon with some paperwork for you."

The doctor walked out.

"How are you feeling?" Jim asked.

"Pretty good," she said. "The doctor said I can go home, but I'll need to rest for a few days."

Erin walked over and gave Jessi a hug. "I thought I was never going to see you again!"

"Jessi returned the hug and said, "You can't get rid of me that easily!" She pushed Erin back and looked at her. "But what about you? How was it that you got tied up in that warehouse anyway?" She glared at Barry and asked, "And where was Barry that whole time?"

"Don't be mad at Barry," Erin said, grabbing his arm and hugging him.

"If it wasn't for him, I probably wouldn't be here right now."

Jessi looked at Barry suspiciously. Barry turned red with embarrassment.

"I just did what I had to do to save my girl," he said modestly.

"Okay. I'll be impressed for this moment," Jessi said. "Now, make this moment last for me, and tell me what you did that was so heroic."

"Well," Barry started, "earlier today, I remembered I had read something about that warehouse. I couldn't remember what it was, but I remembered at the time that something seemed familiar in the story. I couldn't place my finger on it, though. After the incident at the police station, Erin and I had a fight. So I dropped her off at Taco Taco and ran to the library to use their Internet. I searched back in previous newspapers until I found the story. I realized that what seemed so familiar was the owner's name. I knew that he had been in Erin's Kung Fu classes. Erin has recounted the story to me numerous times, and his name was right there, on the edge of my brain, but not so close that I could see it. So I thought that either this guy was good and could maybe help us, or the bad guy. I was hoping he was the good guy."

Erin jumped in, "Anyway, he called me up and said he had some news to help us with this murder mess. He apologized for what happened at the police station and said he wanted to come get me so we could finish working on this together. He said he would meet me outside of the restaurant. That's when I left. But then I saw O'Malley outside, so I called Barry back and told him to meet me on the other side of the building. That's when I ran in, talked to you and Jim, and ran out again. I didn't have time to explain."

"So we drove to the warehouse, and I filled Erin in on the way. What we didn't know was that Jake was following us. I guess he was somewhere by Taco Taco and saw us leave."

"That must have been who was following us this morning," Jim said, "and that explains why he was gone once O'Malley showed up."

Barry continued. "So when we got to the warehouse, we drove to the back where the trucks pulled in to unload and parked. We exited the car, walked to the front, and hid behind bushes. We waited for a long time, then went to the front door and found it was open."

"We went inside and just looked around a little," Erin continued. "Since we didn't see any other cars there, we figured that the killer hadn't arrived yet, and maybe we could set up a trap for him. As we were walking around inside the building, we heard four loud noises outside. Barry told me to stay put and that he would investigate."

Barry said, "I walked outside and didn't see anything or anyone, but when I went back to check on the car, I saw that all four of my tires had been flattened. That's when I knew someone was here. We just hadn't seen him yet. So I ran back to the front and went inside. I looked around, but I couldn't find Erin."

Erin said, "Jake came up behind me when I was waiting for Barry. I never heard him coming. He grabbed under my jaw and started to drag me away. I had no balance or leverage, and I couldn't cry out. I could barely breathe. So, he took me back to the office area, sat me in the chair, and then used a pressure point over a nerve cluster on my neck to make me pass out."

Barry broke in and continued again. "I started looking around. It was creepy. It was all dark, and I couldn't find Erin anywhere. I kept looking and finally heard someone talking. I crept over to where the talking was coming from, and just inside the office door, I saw Erin tied up in a chair. Erin was unconscious, and Jake was ranting and raving. I think he was talking to Erin even though she couldn't respond. He was talking about how he should kill Erin because she was Jessi's best friend. It was bizarre. I thought maybe if I showed up, he would get freaked out and run, so I stepped inside the office door and told him to leave Erin alone. Then he looked at me and smiled. That was the weirdest part. He smiled a big smile and then chuckled a little. He calmly walked over to me, smiling the whole time. I saw his hand move, and that's the last thing I remembered before the cop woke me up. He must have hit me in the jaw because it sure hurts like crazy now!"

"When I woke up, " Erin said, "I tried to reason with Jake. He just rambled about how hurt he was, how he never got over Jessi, and how I was probably the reason that she never liked him. I was terrified because he was just rambling, and it seemed like he was reaching a new level of anger. Then we heard the front door creak a little. It must have been because he's owned the warehouse for so long that he noticed it, but that's when he taped my mouth and slipped out another door. But before he left, he got close to my face and told me how much fun this was going to be and that he would save me for later. Creeped me out."

"Wow! Jessi exclaimed, "What really hit me during all of this was that the voice I heard yesterday was my own. I just didn't recognize it since I was hearing it from outside of my own body. So, I put myself in the very situation I was trying to save someone else from, and yet, there was not someone else. It was me the entire time."

Everyone was quietly looking at Jessi, digesting what she had just said.

"Just accept it," she said.

# CHAPTER 22

## SURPRISES

A few days later, Jessi, Jim, Erin, and Barry were in the sushi restaurant once again. This time, however, they are enjoying themselves, laughing, and telling jokes. While waiting for dinner, the subject returned to the significant event of a few days earlier.

"So Barry," Jessi started, "why were you being so weird the past few days?"

"Oh!" Erin said. "That's right! I didn't tell you." Erin brought her left hand up under Jessi's face. She looked at it and smiled at the ring on her finger.

"He asked you to marry him?"

"And I said yes!" Erin squealed. "He had just closed a deal with a company in Japan. That's why he didn't want the police checking up on him. He thought that police activity right then would mess up the deal. He wanted to propose to me on Saturday, but then the whole murder thing came up, and, well, he didn't feel like it was the right time."

"Barry!" Jim said, "Congratulations!"

"She's my girl," he said shyly. "What can I say?"

A toast was offered, and success was wished to the happy couple.

"Jessi," Erin said, "will you be my maid of honor?"

"I was hoping you'd ask," Jessi said with a smile.

"Hey, Jim?" Barry said. "We've been through a lot during the past twenty-four hours. I don't know if you'd be willing, but would you be my Best Man?"

Jim reached across the table, shook Barry's hand, and said, "It would be an honor."

After the merriment had calmed down, Jim asked Jessi, "So you haven't heard any more sounds?"

"Not a single one," she said.

"Ironic," Erin said.

"What's that?"

"That the guy who did something that caused you to have the ability in the first place was the same person that did something to make it leave," Erin said.

Jessi looked at Erin, "That *is* weird. Maybe it was meant to be because, if you think about it, he actually gave me the means to stop him from killing me."

"Still gives me shivers," Barry said.

"So, do you miss it?" Jim asked.

"What? Hearing future sounds?"

"Yeah."

"Yes and no," Jessi replied, "I mean, I could hear those sounds for so long now that it's something I've gotten used to, like an extra arm or something. Now that it's gone, I'm relieved, and yet it's strange not hearing things that aren't there. I was just starting to get used to it."

"I guess that means it's time to concentrate on the here and now," Jim laughed.

"Guess so," Jessi said and leaned over to kiss Jim.

The waiter brought dinners, and everyone let out "ooohs" and "ahhhhs."

"We should come here every night," Erin said, taking a big bite.

As Jessi took her first bite, she heard a loud crash come from the kitchen with running and then the fading sound of the fire alarm. She looked quietly at everyone else at the table and said, "As much as I love this place, let's eat somewhere else tomorrow night." Jessi smiled to herself and took another bite.

# ABOUT THE AUTHOR

Drew Bankston lives in the Rocky Mountains with his wife, two dogs, and a garden.

Before he started writing science fiction, Drew received his bachelor's degree from Colorado State University. After graduation, he worked various jobs in retail and Asset Protection while working on his writing. He's still working but would eventually like to write full-time and stop working for other people. He loves meeting and speaking with his fans.

For more information or to write to Drew, please visit his website at http://www.drewbankston.com, where you can sign up to receive new book notifications.

www.ingramcontent.com/pod-product-compliance
Lightning Source LLC
Chambersburg PA
CBHW020657120726
47906CB00001B/317